BOW T......

Shadwell park walkabout, couple of things ambling about in my brain, leaning on the handrail looking into the old Thames sloshing about below 'Gord knows what that is' I thought.., as a soggy shape floated past, I don't really, wanna know. Now I'm down this way I'll stroll up the Highway into Cable street then cut through Lukin Street, into Commercial Road and have a chat with someone in my family's church.

A walk my family would have made hundreds of times to School and Church, and after a teaching. Back home to Dunstan's Building's Cable street. Eight Children, and parents, in two rooms. A dockside upbringing for a hardy loving community.

In my aim to be Bone-Fide, I want by way of some purpose in life, to discover from a once bombed out church, now rebuilt,-in fact the Cathedral of East London, namely St Mary And St Michael, the date of my parents wedding and the date of my baptism, we have no records or photos of the happy events, or otherwise, I'm sure everything is kosher so as I'm going back in time I will join the dots of life together, if you don't mind I'll leave the dash's out.

Father Patrick looked up as I walked in through the aisle of the church, the afternoon sun caressing the atmosphere is there a more peaceful feeling? I crossed myself… good boy... I felt my mother's praise,

"How you doing father"?

"Greatly, greatly he said and yourself, is it fine you are, Can I help you in any way?

oh well oh well, its yourself Jake, is it not, well well well."

I explained my interest in my past.

"The blitz, Father, the docks and our homes targeted. Hard times."

"Terrible terrible days, I wasn't here at the time, but I know from the fill'm's, what horror was inflicted on the families, no peace even to pray, as you know our lovely church was bombed,- and some poor souls were killed, god rest our friends and neighbours. There were some records saved, from the bombers I believe, so I've been told. I will ask our office staff so, so I will. If they would kindly trawl through the records to find the documents to make, as you say, a bone fide cockney, but sure, you know you are, and wouldn't I know you are a kosher cockney, an all an all an all". We both laughed at Father Pat's wise but daft explaining.

"Now I've got to see to these kind ladies"

He said as whispering three ladies came into the church. "Can we start work father, is it alright?" they whispered almost in unison.

BOW TALES

DANIEL PATRICK BEAMISH

ISBN 978-1-915292-17-9

Printed in Great Britain by
Biddles Books Limited, King's Lynn, Norfolk

DANBEAMISH @ MSN.COM

"Of course, "he smiled." welcome, welcome, we are finished" he said with a questioning nod to Jake.

"By the way, would it be Jake, Jack, Jesse, I've heard people call you all manner of names, now whatever is your Christian name for goodness sake?"

"Father you can call me anything, as long it's not early in the morning. But its Jesse,-with a surname of Tulip you can imagine the names I got called, so I change it when it suits, for the girls its Jesse Tulip, I think it makes me sound a bit..., you know...what's the word?"..., "Queer?"queried Father Pat.

"No ..d'you mind...esoteric." Jesse said indignantly.

"Well.., Not queer.., but quare, us Irish have a saying, the quare fella, meaning some one who's a bit of a meschigena," Father laughed.

"And.. for the football its Jake, and for work its Jack, after that I don't give a stuff what people call me." I shrugged.

"And why would you. Now I must see to my ladies, bless them, hard workers so they are."

"That should keep you busy for a while right."

I winked.

Father jabbed me on the shoulder playfully.

"Be off with you, you rascal "he smiled.

The ladies were busy dusting the beautiful stature of St Michael the Archangel, the commander of Gods army against Satan, the patron Saint, and the protector of innocent people, he carries the book of Deeds after death, to God for judgement on each and every one of us, the ladies quite naturally were very very gentle and careful,.. you can't be too careful with God about.

"Have you seen the Toke's about lately Father? "I asked… "I won't keep you a minute, just a quickie…" I held my palm up,

He closed one eye looked across to the ladies and St Michael, a thinking nod on his face,… "Now I think Hettie was at mass Sunday… yes, Yes, now I'm sure… I'm thinking she was, a lovely women, so she is. haven't seen Izzy Toke, Jim, that is, for a while, and Connie, well you know what you lads are like" with a questioning nod of his head.

"We won't mention the old man, ah, Father?"

Father Pat laughed. "Meself, and Charlie have had many a barney…fierce angry man, so he is,"

Jesse thought, I'd better get a move on if I want to get around. He shook Fathers hand.

"I've got to be off, up Jubilee street as it happens, a bit of agro with Connie possible.., Father."

"No shenanigans, I hope? "He looked questioningly.

"Connie can be a bit of a twerp, right. I run a local football team, lumping a ball about over Hackney Marsh's. We're in the fifth division of the East London Sunday Morning League."

"Really! would you ever wonder at such fame, such chutzpah." Father said with a saucy grin.

"Honestly, Father, you and your Yiddish talk."

"Following in our father's footsteps, don't you know..,"

Father Pat put his arm around Jesse's shoulder and steered him out through the church doors into Commercial Road, they stood and looked up and down, Father waving to people on the other side of the road.

"Now no schlimazel with Connie" he said

Jesse thought, I won't bother telling Father about Connie throwing a wobbly…all because I mentioned he might make a better job at left back if he took the flat cap off and spat the dog-end out. I better let Father get back to the Ladies in his church. Jesse called over his shoulder as he walked away…

"By the way, Dizzy Gillespie and his band are up Poplar town hall next Saturday,"

"I'll see if I can get some free tickets for that, I do like a good Irish Ceili band. Now when I was in a Irish language school near Falcaragh, Donegal, we used to sneak into town and listen to Paddy Gillespie and his Ceili band in a pub, would that be himself?"

Father asked. "I was a bit of a lad then, got caught netting salmon. Meself…, and a couple of likely lads. John Magee the Bailiff caught us called us some names in Irish, not very nice either.., smacked me round the head. Took the fish and nets, with a warning… holding up his clenched fist.

We skedaddled smartish."

Jesse laughed." No, this man is an American Jazzman"

Father started to walk away. "Would that be like Winifred Atwell's Jazz piano? I quite like that "Father asked.

Jesse thought I'm wasting my time talking about music to Father as he walked away, he shouted back. "Tell me Father have you heard of the Beatles"?

He stopped so he could hear Fathers reply. "Funny you should say that, so it is, that reminds me to get In touch with Ratty Letwin the Bug man, get him to bring his gadgets and potions to church, my customers are getting lots of insect bites from Beatles…did you get bitten as well?"

Jesse waved goodbye to Father Pat, still chuckling, he tried to cross Commercial Road, the road itself runs through the heart of a very proudly independent area of dockside East London, the Cockney tribe who live in the present and are proud of their ancestor from the depressive past retain the humour of the working class, independent.. guyver, bags of swagger, some might say lairey schmoozers, affable, live and let live, but are still an inclusive gawd blimey tribe.

After a couple of aborted tries and the odd swear word mouthed at some drivers, getting back in answer the two finger and the one finger salute, he managed to get to the other side only to trip up the curb, swearing to himself and would have fallen arse over tip, if a middle aged man hadn't caught him and steadied him. The stranger smiled and said "For gawd sake Yossel you slomacky git, look what you are doing, you'll ruin that lovely bit of schmutter"

Jesse breathing heavily said "thanks for that, oh its yourself Abe, is it?" "how are you keeping?"

Abe looked at him quizzically "No you silly twerp get your mincers sorted, It's me Eric, Abe's me brother. Don't thank me, I'm a fool to meself, I should have let you skin your knees, your trousers would have ripped and I'm on hand ready and willing to make you a new pair of strides.am I a wally or what?"

Jesse straightened himself up, reached forward with his both hands and lightly touched Eric's elbows, "Sorry about that, you look alike"

"Course we do," Eric chuckled. I don't know if you noticed, I've got a beard"

Jesse said "Yes I can see that"

"well Abe' hasn't you twerp, oy vey.." Eric said lifting his arms up.

They had to move about the pavement, as people were pushing past. Eric brushed Jesse down, "alright now?" He asked, nodding his head, nice whistle, mohair right? We'd have done it cheaper"

Jesse remembered the last suit he got from Eric and Abe's shop. and he wasn't best pleased. Jesse said he was working on a bombsite in the city so went to a shop there. "How's business? Plenty of shekels?" he asked,

Eric said "I make a living, mustn't grumble. Must dash, look after yourself" as he headed off towards the Troxy theatre, near his shop. "Cheers, mazeltov" said Jesse,

As he made his way in the opposite direction to Eric, up Commercial Road, towards his future barney with Connie, weaving more carefully around the people, and shop goods on the pavement. Jesse chuckled to himself, as a thought popped into his mind, a thought with music, the sound of a barrel organ, just like the scenes in old black and white movies, depicting east London. In the eyes of the director of the movies, smog filled dingy streets, usually an old café with actors in red silly little scarves, ill-fitting flat caps, talking in fake cockney accents, which normally scorch the ears of east Londoners. As Jesse ruminated, so far in his middle twenties, he was still yet to see or hear a barrel organ with or without a monkey with a collecting tin. As he turned into Jubilee street he kept the cockney themed thoughts by singing to himself *'Any old iron, any old iron, any any any old iron, you look neat talk about a treat, you look a dapper from your napper to your feet'. Dressed in style, brand new tile, with your father old green tie on, I wouldn't give you tuppence for your old watch chain, old iron, old iron!*

Why I said I'd do the business for this bleeding team I don't know. Thought Jesse, seemed a good idea at the time.

Me and a few of the local fella's from the Bow Rd manor, got the football bug when we were following West Ham, in their glory years,1964 to 68, and what glory years, we started having a kickabout over Victoria Park, and some bright spark come up with the idea of getting a team up and joining the East London Sunday Morning league, I was nominated to do the necessary, by popular vote, I wasn't there at the time, as it just happened to be one of the times I was living in Stratford, I did used to move about London in different digs, but never went far from Bow Road. I was having agro with a with the misses at the time, so it kept me busy with team business, and mostly out of hostilities on the home front.

Psyching himself up for a ruck with Connie Toke, Jesse thought ain't it bleed'n fair, I'm doing all the bleed'n running about and getting no backup. I wouldn't mind, there's a few of the other lads as big as Connie, the big schmuck. We need the team shirt he's got, I could only get a full teams shirts from the I.L.C. as a grant, no extras. And it took me a full day trolling about County Hall, being passed from one office to another until I got sorted. We need the team shirt Connie's got, if we don't turn up for a match full kit'd out we lose points. He's threatened to give me a doughboy if I turn up at his drum, if it comes to fisticuff, I'll have to use my training at The West Ham Boxing Club, mind that was when I was thirteen...one of my proudest memories was the picture of me and another boy having a photo taken for the Stratford Express paper, with The Lord Mayor of West Ham after giving a boxing exhibition at a church function. front page no less, will it help with a ruck? Only if I'm fly and dirty, my bantam weight against Connie's middleweight, lots of ducking and diving, and fingers in the eyes should do the trick.

He had better be in, he told me when he got a start at Cohens, by Rotherhithe tunnel, that he can be indoors in no longer than ten minutes.

Knocking on the door Jesse had to wait a nervous minute... suddenly the door was yanked open violently. Two pair of antagonistic eyes met like organ stops, then melted when Connie said nervously, "Oh hello Jake...how you doing?" with a flicker of a smile on his face.. Jesse realising with relief Connie was more nervous than himself.

"I'm sweet as a nut ...yourself?"

"nice whistle, mohair annit?" Connie asked

"Tonic mohair, as it happens, got it from Bilgorries by Liverpool Street Station, been working up that way"

A female voice shouted from the back of the dark hallway... "Is that that Tulip pratt?. If your gonna have a ruck, don't do it on the doorstep I've just red leaded it"

Connie shrugged his shoulders and put a what can I do look on his face. "And tell him to stick his poxy shirt and his poxy team up his arse. instead of wasting Sunday losing every week over Hackney Marshes you should be helping the old man up the allotments. Oh and by the way ...tell the Tulip to get a move on and buy a new shovel to replace the bleed'n one he broke, your Dad's not stopped moaning about it, he's led us a dog's life"

Connie gestured with his thumb over his shoulder and raised his eyes. "Sorry about that, once she starts, she don't stop, the old cow."

"I was going to bring the shirt round, but one of the boys said you'd moved."

Jesse shouted over Connie's shoulder, into the dark hallway "Sorry Mrs Toke, I'll put the shovel at the top of my...to do list..," and grinned at Connie".

Ominous silence from the dark hallway was broken by a snort, then..." Oh top of your, to.. do. ..list, is it? You saucy little fecker..?"

Jesse and Connie laughed, quietly.

"Fecker? Where did that come from, fecker?"

Jesse laughed shaking his head.

Connie answered. "She picks up all the odd Irish saying from Maggie O'Connell, her best friend, you know, a big family of em, right."

Jesse couldn't help thinking that Mrs Toke was one peculiar women, a right cockney, but at a party, her and Izzy do a turn, where she makes out she's a barber shaving a customer and plasters Izzy's face with shaving cream while singing the aria from The Barber Of Seville in German, while Izzy's squirming about making out she's cut his ear's or his nose off.

Quite a few stage acts have a stab at it.

He's a nutcase is Izzy, anything for a laugh.

Strange old family the Tokes.

"Your mother Connie…, if you don't mind me saying is…a bit peculiar, aint she? A Cockney who knows opera."

"She ain't me real Mother. My real Mum was killed in an air raid.

The old man was in Germany, in the army.

I was brought up by me Aunt's until the old man was demobbed. It was a bit of a shock for the family when he turned up with Hettie. I was only a kid at the time, you know what it was like then, she was just another lady who would care for us kids like their own, cuddle or clump, we were all one big family.

She's good as gold to us, her and the old man do have big rucks, he says he should have left her in the knocking shop where he found her, he can be a right maggot at times."

Hettie, withdrew into the kitchen at the back of the house, leaving the boy's to they're gasing.in her mind's eye she was back in time. (*With her mother's aura, daydreaming, the warm* encompassing all embracing mother's unfailing love…

(Are you well, My Liebling?…)

I am safe and happy Mutter, my life here is a joy every day I can breathe peace and freedom thank god.., thank god for English Samaritans.

Momma I feel guilty for not helping you and Poppa more.

I am grateful to Poppa for putting me in The Fiesta Nightclub. Munich suburbs. I was an excellent cleaner thanks to you Momma.

The girls protected me, bless them like a little sister, I was so young.

(Our joy is your safe. That is all we wish.)

Danke Momma.

Mutti…I have been a bit of a rascal in my new life. I might need to unburden my soul…, and confess sometimes…, and ask you to forgive any sins I've committed. As my creator…, only you can give me absolution.

(Hettie Liebling, as your Mother I forgive you anything.)

Hettie whispered as she came out of her daydream"

Danke schone Mutter, auf wiedersehen darling god bless.")

"She is very clever, is Hettie, knocks spots of all of us." Connie explained.

"She said as soon as she got herself settled, she would be like all the local women,

She would walk and talk the same. Fortunately, Maggie O'Connell took her under her wing, she's got four daughters', so one more was no trouble.

Maggie got her to study a catechism, a little catholic book, gave her different numbers of the sayings in it, picked up English no problem. Now she can f and blind with the rest. Hettie does come out with the odd Irish saying that she picks up from Maggie. Talking about the O'Connell's, Izzy copped a right hander from Norah when he got saucy with her, he had a black eye for a week, he wore it with pride, thought it was funny.

Good job she didn't tell her brothers, if she had, he'd have been able to add the old song, *Two lovely black eye's oh wot a*

*surprise, all for telling a girl, I like her dumpling and pies. Two
lovely black eyes. To his repertoire.*

Once Connie got his talking hat on he didn't stop.

"That's how we found out about the two Arabs who had
Sweets Sweetmans shop. Do you remember the other year when
those pair of Lascar were fished out of the Thames at Millwall?

"Yeah funny old business that was, wasn't it"? Jesse said.

"Well the cops kept the lid on it. The official story from them
was the two Lascar fell off one of the ships being unloaded by
Free Trade Wharf, and drowned."

"What we know and they didn't want to know, is they
wasn't Lascars but the two brothers from Sweetmans shop and
what's more they weren't Lascars but Indians, who wangled
there way here after the war, they turned up in Stepney, East
London claiming to have been in the British Indian Army, and
had been prisoners in a camp in Heuberg in Germany. There
were a lot of displaced people about, and nobody checked.

The pair opened Sweetmans old shop selling grocery's. Poor
old Sweets, he called himself Sweets after an American jazz

trumpeter called Sweets Edison. Well Morry Sweetman, that was his proper name, He used to run a local jazz band, well his lip went and he couldn't play with his band anymore, so he sold up and retired to Canvey island."

Connie in full yacking mode explained.

The door to the shop was open and Hettie in her usual way stood quietly. About five foot four in height. Her fair hair permed, neatly dressed with a high necked jumper and cardigan, navy blue trousers, low heeled shoes. A silver cross and chain around her neck. Delicate plump features. Walked in to get some groceries.

Abdul, a dark balding Asian man, aged in his fifties, small statured. Wearing a grey linen jacket, dark trousers and a green coloured bow tie standing behind the shop counter, with his back to Hettie, was shouting angrily at the back store room,

"Dumcofe, schvinehund idiot. Do you want to be back in Heuberg, or knowing you…you'd probably prefer.. Oldebroek".

Tarik hidden in the back room, shouted "Es wa nicht meine schuld... Ya.. Oldebroek, danke bitte…, you fucking native." Hettie cottoned on straight away about the two them. She was born in Stetten, and worked in a nightclub as a general help, in the outskirts of Munich, Were she met Dad. She said those towns were where Hitlers, Indian Regiment, The Tiger Legion, were stationed.

Abdul shouted back

"It was.. your fault" turned, saw her, and shouted to his brother.

"We have a charming lady in the shop, be quiet Tarik."

Then to Hettie, "I'm sorry about that, did you understand any of our chatter?"

He moved about the counter tidying the bacon slicer and till and greaseproof wrapping paper, whilst smiling at Hettie, sleazily.

"Only… when we're having a row we sometimes slip into our native lingo."

Hettie said the other one, Tarik, came in from the back store room. He was a younger lighter skinned man around late thirties in age, with a Tony Curtis style hair cut, the same linen jacket as his brother, but smarter shirt, and trousers, and started getting all smarmy.

Its Mrs Toke is it not? He looked at his brother, and nodded in her direction,

"She always looks so nice and fresh,"

who nodded in agreement.

"You know if you ever need to put goods on tick we don't mind, for our best customers." Hettie had heard the odd whisper about what they expect if anybody gets in schtuk to them.

Abdul then said they must get out and about. We're stuck in here, day after day. And a day on the river would be great.

And did she know anybody with a row boat.

They'd love to paddle on the Old Thames, get some fresh air.

Hettie said to them that she did know a fellow, known locally as woggle eyed Gordon Fipps.

He does a bit of mooching around the docks, he might lend you his rowboat.., cost you I'd say. Lives round about Shadwell Park.

We'd be very grateful if you could show us. Said Tarik, perhaps, if you like you could come out in the boat with us? what do you say, Abdul?

What a good idea. We would love it if you could. You know you could trust us, we would make sure of your safety we can swim, Can you Mrs Toke?

Hettie handed her grocery list to, Abdul and caught the of conspiratorial look between the two. She said they looked positively evil.

Abdul glanced at the list. Sorry we're out of liver and bacon today, but we can get it special for you tomorrow. Sorry about that. But if you can come in tomorrow we'll make sure its in. If you could show us where that chap with the boat lives.., Mr Pipps was it? Hettie giggled, Gordon Fipps. She told him. Well Mr Fipps, he smiled. Well if you could show us we'd give you the liver and bacon as a treat from us.

Hettie excused herself from the shop and went home to cook the dinner.

Charlie, Connie and for a change Izzy, were busy eating her dinner, Goulash, a Hettie special. When she told them about the business with the two brothers in Sweetmans, the locals still called it Sweetmans, despite Morry being gone a few years.

Connie said him and a few of the boys will get the oily rats.

"Charlie shook his head, no you won't, if Hettie's right? And if anybody knows, she would. And I remember when I was out there, there were lots of rumours about Hitlers' foreign troops. The pair of them could be classed as traitors. The old Bill might be interested..then again. The cops reckon they're run off their feet. Most of them are a bunch of tossers. To busy nicking the fella's at Bow Road Underground Station with a carrier bag of firewood. They done Alfie Sudsy the other week.

He got saucy and said it was a Chippendale Whatnot, he found in a bin, in a hundred bits, and he was going to stick it together again. An idiot Beak done him a tenner for stealing an antique.

So the pair want to go out in Woggly Gordon's boat? Ah… Izzy glanced at Hettie, I've a good mind to drill a hole in it."

Charlie lifted his hand up and raised a finger from side to side. "No, no. Let me think on it."

"I tell you what, I know where old goggle eye drinks." said Izzy." I'll have a word with him."

Charlie exclaimed." Don't be a pratt all your life, don't say anything to him, the man's a right shyster. But you could go and see him and arrange to get his boat. Then Hettie can tell the Indians. We don't want them getting windy and skedaddling before we shop them.

Early evening drinker's in the snug bar in the Old Rose pub, The Highway, were scarce.

Woggle Eyed Gordon in his usual corner, in the dark, nursing the dregs of a pint of black and tan. Izzy peering through the gloom bumped into the table Gordon had his elbows resting on.

"You clumsy git, what's a matter with you?"

"Its me.., Izzy Toke, sorry about that."

"I can see its you, you always was a slomacky sod..., what d'you want?"

"I tell you what I wanted to see you about..you know your boat?"

"Ye...s?" Woggle eyed Gordon suspicion's aroused, he looked one eyed at Izzy who explained why.

Gordon rubbed his thumb and forefinger together, Izzy gave him a fiver, and was told where to get the boat.

He got back later that evening and gave the details to the Toke family.

"It cost me a fiver y'know?" Charley waved at him impatiently.

"Alright alright.. well.. Gordon said go to Shadwell Park, walk down Glamis Road by the side of the park and look out on the left, for Shadwell stairs, the boat is tied up at the bottom, named Dora. Take the tarpaulin off and fold it and put it in the boat, so you don't lose it, make sure the oars are alright, untie the boat and away you go. Make sure you pack everything back the way you found them when your finished, tie it back to the iron ring on the wall, I'll expect you to pay for a new boat if its damaged."

Charley looked at Hettie. "All you got to do is tell the two Indians what Izzy just told us."

After a visit to the shop and arranging to meet them on the corner of Shadwell Park in the afternoon, after they closed their shop, and show them to where the boat was kept. Hettie explained it would cost them ten pounds for the hire, and ten pounds for a deposit. Abdul grumbled about the money, but Taric was all smiles. We'll have a good time, yes, he winked at Hettie, who nodded back. She gave a wave and walked out of the shop.

"Do you think she understood any of the German she heard?" Taric asked.

"Not a chance" Abdul answered" You know them round here to ignorant.., don't understand our Indian accent, let alone German, some of the Jews would.., but she's not Jewish, she had a cross around her neck. She looked to stupid anyway.., but in any case…? Abdul looked at his younger brother fondly "We've done plenty of worse things to get this far, and haven't been caught, we're far to clever for these, pigs, one more won't matter, we will get to our homeland, I will make sure of that brother,"

The terrible horrors of war across Europe they experienced, blanked any sympathetic decency towards local people.

We'll work out the best way to deal with them. Now don't blab it about, right, Connie?

Who nodded.

"Izzy.., you didn't say anything to Woggle eye? No.., Not really, he's away with the Fairies, anyway, you know what he's like. He's too busy fishing the stiff's out of the Thames for the old Bill, save them getting their great plates wet, bless er'm."

Hettie asked if that was right about Gordon, Izzy told her the family have been fishing corpses out of the Thames for generations. Hettie shivered, how horrible.

Now mind what I said, keep shtum until I work it out."

"Yes okay Miss Marples," Izzy said sarcastically.

My old pal Morry needs to hear about this…, Morry of all people, thought Izzy.

He thought of the good times Morry and himself had, in the pubs around East London. He'd turn up wherever Morry's Band were playing, with his carrier bag of props, the fairy wand and the long women's bloomers. Him and Morry took it in turns to perform

'No One loves a Fairy over forty'.., and Morry, his Poppas favourite.., Yiddle on the Fiddle. His Poppa was a great joker, they'd usually do a couple of Sophie Tucker saucy songs, getting the place warmed up. Izzy always had to do his comedy song, with the long bloomers on.., You cant beat the old Fleecy lined.

The memory of those nights reflected in the back of Izzy's mind when he phoned Morry and told him what was happening at his old shop. Morry said he would get in touch with the right people, and leave it in their hands.

Well Connie said, "that's the full S.P on the two nazi.., A.,rabs,"

He took a deep breath, "like a bleed'n book at bedtime"

Jesse laughed, "you can say that again."

Connie handed the disputed shirt to Jesse.

He shouted over his shoulder, "I'm going Mum."

"Thank gawd for that, its bleed'n freezing in here." As she slammed the door.

The boys walked down past the terrace houses in Jubilee Street towards Stepney Way.

"Oi hold up, you pair of poofs"

A dark lad shouted as he ran up behind them.

They stopped and welcomed Vince slapping him on the shoulders. A hefty twenty four year old man, crinkly black cropped hair, about five nine in height, puffing.

"Your blowing a bit, you be alright for a game Sunday?" Asked Jesse.

"Yea I'll be fine. Got early starts, aint I, doing a bit of contracting on a site over the water, round the Oval, near Brixton, blimey you want to see the spades over there. I've had rucks galore.., saucy barstards' got the cheek to ask me where I'm from.., I'm a fucking Cockney born and bred like all my family, so stick that up your arse, we belong here.., and I give them the threatening look my old man give's anybody who's got the guts to say something sarcastic to him."

The boys stood nodding sympathetically.

"I know what you mean Vince, "said Connie "They're so effin loud and lairey."

"Connie's just been telling me about the business with them two arabs in Sweetmans shop"

said Jesse shaking his head.

Vince held his hand up and explained how the family had to stand in front of his Father to stop him going out of their house and strangling the pair when he heard about it. He was here during the bombing, I was born at the end. He lost his best friend. It was a blessing when we heard. They had disappeared. He was chuffed when he heard the local yobs had raided the shop, although he would have given any of my brothers or sister a hiding if we had taken anything from the shop. No identification about the brothers was found by the police in the shop and the police didn't bother looking. They just asked Hettie if she knew anything, as she had been seen near the park talking to them. She said she directed them down to Shadwell Stairs and left them. The police had a word with Charlie saying, tell your missus to forget about everything to do with the brothers, and emphasizing they were two laskers who fell off a ship, a pat on the shoulder, probably stowaways, you know what I mean they added.., know what we mean?

"You reckon someone topped em?"

Vince asked.

Connie nodded, "certainly looks iffy don't it."

"Where are you off to?" Vince asked

"I'm off to find me old man," and looking at Vince.., "What about you?" Jesse asked.

"Home…Where you off to, Con? somewhere nice?."

"Nosy little bleeder aint, ya." Connie said laughing to Vince.

The boys walked down towards Whitechapel High Road chatting about their nights delights. Jesse told them he was hoping to catch up with his father in one of a couple of pubs at Bow Bridge opposite the Civic Centre, The Bird In Hand, the old man's regular boozer, or possibly The Bow Bells.

He hoped he could get him a start on one of the Iron Fighting Gangs he managed.

Vince said he'd better get home to his family's terraced home, he shared with his wife and baby, his parents, and younger brother and sister. I've been up at the council, but no chance of a council flat. Connie said I tried that, the gits wouldn't even put my name on the waiting list, what with the shortage left over after the war, and them idiot slum clearance planning prats, knocking good houses down. Just like the house's the boys were walking passed.

Jesse said he hoped to see the boys up the Aberdeen pub Saturday night, started the boys reminiscing. A laugh a minute with Gaye Travis, and his chums he chuckled, his introductions are great.

"It's me In person, the one and only, extra-terrestrial Gaye Travis.., Gaye by name, by nature…? Compere extraordinaire..?

Erm…um?don't we all,?" A lift of one manicured eyebrow and a wink. "A bit of gentleman's relish? don't we all sweety." Gaye held his arms out wide…" And here he is…, Huh, Huh, H, Aitch' The Whore of Hackney. And his advertising song.

Old Gaye called across a lady who lived over the road, It's big enough to ride,

He took her down his garden path and showed her it with pride,

When she saw the size of it, the excited lady cried,

ALL TOGETHER, COME ON, LET'S HAVE YEAH,

Oh what a beauty, I've never seen one as big as that before,

Oh what a whopper, so big and round and fat,

And a lovely colour....green.

Connie laughed, the whore of Hackney in his mini-skirt, stocking and suspenders, is a scream, he always is, a case and half.

Vince piped up, sounds like he's got a bit of a fan here, winking at Jesse.

And the big old whack with the string of pearls and flowery hat. Gaye introduced.

Now for a bit of refinement the so so sophisticated and oh so posh the darling of the upper class, the lower class any effin class, her ladyship, The Duchess, to sing, oy vey,

'Bei Mir Bist Du Schon.'

The Duchess of Argyle was funny, gawd knows how he gets away with it.

Now two for the price of one, Gaye introduced

Christine, and Mandy, two's up if you like, and who doesn't? Singing Sisters.

Connie said the pair of poofs playing Mandy and Christine were putting it about a bit as well.

The boys laughed and joked at the actions of the talent and good times they had in the Aberdeen pub by Victoria Park, Old Ford,

When they got to Whitechapel Waste. Jesse and Vince caught a 25 bus to Bow Road.

Connie strode off to get himself a bite in Lyons Diner and said ta'tar.

Connie said he met a Sort in the Wimpey bar at Aldgate, the other Sunday when he was up Petticoat Lane. She's studying at a law firm in the City, a foreigner, German, looks rather tasty, wants to see the real East End, she's a decent sort, so I said I'd meet her in the Blind Beggars. She said she's studying criminal law, so I thought the villains in the Blind Beggars would be a good insight into the cockney life.

Once the boys got themselves on the top deck amongst the faggers. Vince asked, "How does he pick up these birds?" "it's not his brains, that's for sure", Jesse answered "I suppose it's because the ladies do find him attractive, lucky bleeder, they reckon he looks a bit like Michael Caine, can't see it myself, looks more like his old man, Charlie." Jesse sniggered. Vince laughed, "Or gawd help us, Uncle Izzy.

He's got fair hair like Michael Caine, not as tall...I think Michael Caine is well over six feet...Apart from that Con's got two left feet, never be a footballer while he's got a hole in his arse, as you well know". Observed Vince laughing.

"Blimey I'd look like Michael Caine if I wasn't a bit dark, with black curly hair, and a bit taller than five eight...And come to that you'd look like Michael Caine,...Jesse,..if you was about a foot taller, at least the same colour hair. "Vince said punching him playfully on the shoulder.

"But there's one thing we've got in common…" Jesse said.. "We've all got cockney accents"

The boys parted at Bow Road Underground Station, Vince promised to turn out on Sunday morning over Hackney marshes for the team, god willing. Jessie carried on the bus until the Civic Centre.

Connie suited and booted in his silver grey Mohair suit with blue silk tie, winkle picker shoes was looking to impress, glancing at his, and his dates reflection in the pubs mirrors he thought proudly how tasty he looked, and her as well, course. He had met Lena Monkstein outside The Blind Beggars. She was dressed in a mini skirted suede suit, neat bobbed fair hair, long brown boots, five six in height. Lena was being eyed

admiringly. He went into full smarmy overdrive, trying his best to look like he was very much at home, amongst the posing mostly other jack the lads, and their birds. When a pub gets a reputation, when you waltz in,.. look the business. Connie eased his way up to the bar, guiding Lena to a bit of elbow room at the bar. Ordering a pint of Lager for himself and a white wine for Lena, they took in the atmosphere, surprisingly pleasant Smokey beery cosy smell.

The evening date together had a very friendly, promising relationship. It was an almost mutual attraction meeting, not obviously of minds, just looks, bearing Connie's lack of guyver or dazzle in the old thinking department, slow on the uptake, a wally, easily led, happy to be led, much to his fathers' annoyance.

In the next few courting weeks, Connie enjoyed Lena's company more warmly. He himself wouldn't say lovingly, not his style right, well. would Michael Caine? Lena had the benefit of an expert tour of Connie's exciting heady times of East London. A trip up the Petticoat Lane, and a carton of Jellied Eels with a knob end of bread, from Tubby Isacc, is a must. To Connie's amazement Lena had no trouble in enjoying them. The other delights Fish and Chips, she liked, who doesn't Connie said, but Pie and Mash with liquor, she would have to get used to, especially eating in a glazed tiled pie shop. Not the sort of restaurant a future Lawyer would dine in, but it's funny how love sends the head doolallytap. Who would have thought a plank like Connie could pull a bird like Lena. Rock music or small group easy listening Sinatra Ella, Tony Bennet style.in plenty of pubs. The gay gay talent in the Aberdeen, the mad mad show band in the Ironbridge Tavern, she happened to be in there when one Friday night the band played Black Sabbath for the last hour, with smoke effect. Nobody was buying drinks, caught up in the thrill of it. Queenie Watts, the owner, and part time Cockney Actress, popped up behind the bar, waving a meat cleaver from the kitchen at the band, shouting..," Cut. Cut.. you bunch of tossers" The noise from them and smoke machine, meant they couldn't see or hear her. And it was to packed for her to barge through. The last hour, known as the eleven o'clock swill, when the tills are at their busiest. Everybody had a good night. Not Queenie...

The band were about to get a good old right royal cockney bollocking from Queenie, they would be advised to take to the hills. Whilst Lena enjoyed the life, of a pubbster. She managed to drag Connie for a day out in Greenwich Park, culturing, and nice walk along Cable Street, not the most scenic walk it must be said, but it's our manor. At it's end, the Royal Mint, a stroll around the Mint and.. The jewel of the East End. Tower Bridge and.. The Tower Of London…Magnificent Majestic.

Hettie told Connie to invite his new lady friend home to dinner. Roast Pork and veg, Apple pie and custard, a normal Sunday dinner, after Mass. Hettie went with her normal Mass partner, Maggie O'Connell. The rest of her family always found some excuse to miss Mass…but not miss dinner. During the boys usual joke's and the chat during dinner, Connie mentioned how good Lena's English is. Charlie spoke about his time in Germany and the place's he was in. Lena asked Hettie where she came from. I'm from a tiny village in the country called Etten, I don't remember much about it because Ich Vater took me away to a safer, he thought…place. I vaguely remember the hills. That's a coincidence Lena said, I wasn't born till much later but I thought I have heard my parents talk about a relative from that area, Greta Lutz…does the name mean anything? Hettie shook her head.., fraid not.

I was about twelve when Dad took me away from the area, because of all the soldiers of every kind everywhere. And I worked in a bar as a skivvy. Just outside the centre of Munich. Uncle Max the owner was a distant relative of some kind, it was very kind of Uncle Max, unfortunately he didn't survive the war and the bombing of Munich. That's where Charlie found me, thank God.

It was a desperate time for me but Charlie, bless him, got into his stroppy nature and insisted he was going to marry me. The army tried to stop us. But he can be awkward bugger when he likes...so that's how I am a...gawd blimey cockney, and proud of it.

"Now come on you lot let's give Lena a treat, you got your bellies full...time for our anthem."

Hettie starts singing, nodding to the others and flicking her open hands to encourage them.

"Maybe it's because I'm a Londoner that I love
London town".

Charlie and Izzy join in, Connie just mouths.

Hettie smiles and winks at Lena.

"Dass ich London Liebe,
Dass ich an sie denke, wohin auch gehe,
I get a funny feeling inside of me,
Just walking up and down,
Vielleicht ist esso wiel ichein,
Londoner bin,
Dass ich London Liebe"
Lena and Connie cuddle laughing.
And for my old Kosher mucker, Morrie. Izzy sings,
"Afshr es iz vaylikh bin a Londoner,
Az ikh libe London taun"
Hettie, Izzy and Charlie harmonise horribly,
"Get orf me barra"

Just an old fashion Sunday after dinner.

Hettie started clearing the dinner plates away. "No no no" Lena exclaimed, "come on Connie move your arse" and she grabbed his arm and pulled him up.

"Nice one Lena make the lazy little git, do some work". Laughed Charlie, "Your learning fast gell, get him at it."

Lena waved at Hettie to sit down. "we'll do the tidying and washing up. You just relax. it's the least we can do after a lovely dinner".

Hettie sat down in an armchair in the corner of the kitchen smiling to herself and breathed the sigh of a very contented Mutti.

Izzy lights up a players' cigarette, offers the packet to Charlie who shakes his head dipping in to his pocket lifting out his tobacco tin, and rolls a cigarette for himself and lights up.

Hettie's mind drifts off into her favourite daydreams of chats with her long departed Mother. Imagination took control.

The vivid image of her mothers' warm smiling face, and the all-embracing aura at having her mother so close, take's Hettie…, despite the chatter of her family…

Completely inside her whole being.

(Mutti liebling your looking wonderful.)

(How are you Engel, schatz.).

(Angel, treasure…, gives me such joy to hear those words again.., Mutti) Hettie in her mind's eye feels her mother's kiss and warm breath on her cheek, it takes her back into such a loving memory a tear lingers in her eye like an eternal treasure.

Charlie laughing and coughing at the same time can't break the spell as Hettie smiles but doesn't hear a word.

(Mother I hope you can help me. I have a big secret…)
(Sube, sweetie, Your mother keeps your secrets on sacred trust, I would never reveal our secret it will never ever be broken.)

(This secret is.., I have rid our world of two Indian brothers who were part of Hitlers nazi army, their troop were called The Tiger legion)

(Did you do something horrible then darling? I cant believe my Hettie would do anything nasty, not my Sube)

(No not awful Mutti, liberating. The two brothers were spreading their evil amongst my people here, as if their crimes weren't bad enough in Germany and France, in fact probably everywhere)

(But darling what an earth have you done? It can't be that bad. I don't think you could have done anything terrible you were always so gentle and kind. That's why you were bullied at school, being to tender hearted)

(Body and soul I've changed Mutti.., not heart darling, the incident needs to be out of my soul and mind and with your forgiveness my sin is forgiven then forgotten)

(My liebling any sin you think might have done would of course be forgiven. Now tell your Mutti everything)

(I went into their shop one morning. They didn't hear me come in; they were shouting at each other in German. They stopped when they saw me and asked if I understood what they were saying, I shook my head and said no. They then told me they were speaking in Arabic. I shrugged my shoulders and said oh, disinterestly. I heard them mention some places like Oldenbroek that triggered my memory from when I was working in the Fiesta Club, hearing some of the different soldiers chatter. They started to get all smarmy, said I could have my shopping on the book, and pay when I was able. I heard what the pair wanted if you got in debt to them, mind you, you would expect nothing less from some of the scrubbers who were always hanging around them, like Bumbussel Flo, and Titsalena Bumsquash, they're known as the local bikes, they live in the same block of flats in Cable Street, just handy to connive with the Indians. The brothers were known as a pair of snidey schnorrers. As Izzy called them, so I smiled at them looking innocent. While they were getting my groceries they were whispering, glancing at me looking shifty. Abdul the older one asked me if I knew anybody local who had a boat, as they would like to go out on the Thames, they said it was a favourite pastime in their own country, he looked at his brother, what do you think Taric?

Great idea Taric answered, and perhaps Mrs Toke would like to have a nice boat ride, it is Mrs Toke isn't it?

Smiling from one to the other.

I left the shop minus liver and bacon, they promised to get me the next day as they were out of it.

Promising to find out about a boat for them.

I had no doubts about what crafty plan they intended, because of their reputation in Oldenbroek where they were wanted for their filthy doings.

I went straight back and told my Charlie The family had a council of war. It was decided that Izzy go to see a bloke they call Woggle eye Gordon, he's well known for mooching about the dock area in his row boat looking for anything that ain't nailed down.

Charlie told me once they arranged about the boat, just to tell the brothers what they were to do and where to go, and leave the rest to Charlie, he would sort the bastards.

I went in the next morning to the brothers shop to pick my shopping, they greeted me with,' wie geht es ihnen', I looked at Abdul blankly, then Taric behind me 'snarled, fairschwinden zee' and I acted startled. I turned looking mystified, Taric smiled smarmily sorry if I startled you. Did you manage to get a boat?

I've arranged the boat, so if you don't mind I can meet you by Shadwell Park in the afternoon about two, and I'll show you where it is.., if I can find it…Gordon Phipps said the tide will be in. If that's alright…I was all smiley, just like they were acting. I've got your card marked, you shits. They tried to catch me out, saying in German, how are you? then snarling.., go away.

(Mutti darling, once they thought I couldn't understand their plans they chattered away how to get rid of me, it was frightening but I kept my nerve, and just smiled.

The sneering hatred in their eyes, and the disgusting hate filled words of spiteful racists, turned my stomach.

Mother forgive me if I let rip, I must call those schnorrers!.. arschlochs!., schwfinehund!.. pieces mist!)

(naughty, naughty, tut, tut) Hettie could imagine her Mother wagging her finger scolding, but smiling.

(Sorry Mutti but they were very evil willing tools of the Nazi's)

Hettie was dressed in a knee length green flared dress. She met the two brothers on the corner of Shadwell Park and Glamis Road.

They were dressed in old shirts and trousers.

(Mutti, you know I was taking my life in my hands.

I heard them whispering in a mixture of German and Arabic as we walked down to the boat. They still didn't cotton on that I could understand them.

So I know they were going to do me in, just in case I did understand them.)

(You took an awful chance darling with two men in a boat.., men like that. Have you been swimming there?)

(If you remember we used to go swimming in a small lake when I was small with your friend Ada. Poplar Baths' is only around the corner and I used to go swimming with Maggie O'Connells' daughter Mary, you would like her mother, she's a lovely girl)

I didn't tell my Charlie as he told me never go near the Thames.

The currents are treacherous and drag you under in seconds. He said his Dad, old Charlie fell in while he was in the docks on Free Trade Wharf.

It took five dockers to drag him out, he was so angry at falling in, and what with John Quarrell standing there laughing at him he had a fight with Squarral, John's nickname. That is John all over, you know what he is like.

Fierce argumentative man, wouldn't stop laughing at old Charlie trying to fight in sopping wet clothes. Every time the old man swung a punch John easily ducked and the old man staggered over.

The three of them were all smiles and chat and made their way around the side of the park to Shadwell Dock Entrance, and found Woggle eyed Gordons boat Dora, at the bottom of Shadwell Stairs.

The boat was tied up back and front to an iron ring on the wall each end.

They pulled the cover off folded it.

Hettie climbed carefully into the boat and sat on the first seat, pushed the cover underneath, she put the oars each side of her.

Hettie ushered the brothers to get in the front. Abdul manoeuvred past Hettie with his hands sliding along the dock wall and grabbed the top of the ring keeping the boat steady. Taric worked his way on the outside and stood beside him trying to keep his balance as the boat rocked. Facing Hettie. They were giggling, laughing.

Chattering in Arabic, rocking the little boat against the dock wall.

Abdul saying careful.., Taric.., careful you Schweich Kopf.

(Now pretty lady, Abdul said to me, Mutti.., with a slimy sickly smirk, enough to turn your stomach.)

We are out of sight below the railing along the park. We find that if we are nice to our customers with treats, they can be very friendly with us.

We will be the same with you, are you game? Taric, sneered are you up for a bit of fun?

The English Fraus schmutzig tortchens, tell us they find our dark skin sexy.

Aint that right Abdul?

Just the right words in our lingo, for English ladies, schmutzig tortchen. Said Abdul.

Do you like our dark skin pretty lady? leaning his face down into Hettie.

I suppose so, she shyly said. Well I could do with some nice things from your shop, and if you keep it a secret.., well, I could do with some fun…she looked from one to the other smiling.

Abdul grinning of course, of course.., right Taric? Who answered enthusiastically, trying to keep his balance and holding on to Abduls left arm, his right hand getting ready to undo the boat from the rope holding ring, Taric giggling. Abdul barked, keep still doof.

Hettie feeling bolder and empowered, almost wanton.

I will have to see what I'm letting myself in for…so to speak.

Pointing to their trousers she said. Drop em,

They looked at each other and shrugged, with Abdul holding on to the ring on the dock wall.

He said Taric.., undo my top buttons on my trousers. With the boat rocking wildly, still holding on to the iron ring with his right hand, he managed to help Taric undo his top buttons. The brothers were enjoying every minute of this escapade as their trousers were shrugged down to their ankles'.

Standing there holding on to each other grinning, in their grubby baggy underpants, laughing along with Hettie.

She told Abdul to undo the rope holding the boat at the iron ring he was holding.

We can move along the docks away from prying eyes, won't do for us to be seen at it, she said winking, at them.

Come on, Taric said, we're ready let's have a shufty…leering.., flicking his hand and fingers up, and looking at the bottom of Hettie's dress.

With the boat undone at the front.

Hettie stood up and slowly lifted her dress up waist high.

The two brothers stared open mouthed and were pointing and laughing in hysterics.

She dropped her dress, picked up the right hand oar lifted it above her head and smashed Abdul on the side of his head, he tried to move out of the way but as he was near the dock wall he barged into Taric and they both fell out away from the dock wall into the Thames.

Hettie was now in full control, she had never felt so aggressive, the abuse she had endured in her country, and the anger she had for foreigners who abused her own people her treasured cockney family all my brethren.

She did not realise how vicious she could be and terrifying. She had no pity, as for once, she acted as she Knew these two intended to do the same to her…as they had done to others.

Taric surfaced first grabbing the side of the boat. Hettie smashed the oar down on his hand hearing the bones break. He shrieked at Hettie open mouthed as he went under, Abdul grabbed onto his brother, with the top of his head just above the water, Hettie brought the oar viscously down on his head.

The two brothers were floundering, Hettie pushed them under, with the oar, they slowly rose again. The Thames was like a whirlpool, then slowly.. slowly..they sank, a few bubbles and swirls drifted up.

Hettie sat back in the boat with a deep sigh, to collect her thoughts.

She looked around the Thames as the tide slowly pulled at the boat, still tied to at the back to the first iron ring. Late afternoon was a quiet time dockside. Nobody was taking any notice.

She pulled herself back to Shadwell Stairs by the rope tied to the boat and the dock wall.

Hettie dropped the revenging oar into the Thames and scrambled back with some difficulty out of the boat and onto Shadwell stairs. Untying the boat she let the tide take it out to presumably follow the bodies towards Millwall and possibly end up at Canvey Island.

Hettie made her way slowly up Shadwell Stairs out into Glamis Road and walked into Shadwell Park.

The stillness of park life brought a sob to her throat.

Making her way around Rotherhithe Tunnel airduct Rotunda, she leant on the railings overlooking the Thames with tears of relief.

Looking down on the Thames she walked along holding onto the railings, all the time looking down in case horror upon horror the brothers surfaced.

She reached the corner of the park and made her way home to cook a special dinner. Hettie's thoughts seeking a Mother's love.

(Mutti darling can you understand my motives
For my terrible actions? I hope you can forgive me, and help ease my conscience? Please Mother, please)

(Engel, Schatz, Hettie if you tell me it was all for the best, that is all I need to know, my Angel my Treasure. You know when you used to tell me your stories and wonderful tales I used to wonder how you could invent such complicated stories, and you were so young, and so imaginative, so so clever.

Hettie do you think you could have imagined, what you would have liked to do to those two...?)

(It was a while back Mother...)

Giggling and laughter brought Hettie back to reality.

Lena asked a question with many answers.

"What is Cockney meaning?"

"That's a good one gell," said Charlie, fag dangling from the side of his mouth.

Izzy laughing blusters, "Blimey.!!"

Connie sniggers, "Gotcha there you professional
Pair of Cockney toe rags."

"Connie Toke, don't be rude to the old pot and pan," Hettie said and joins in laughing.

Charlie describes A Cockney..." First of all the word stems from cocks egg...a wonky egg said to be laid by a cock bird.

Or a wimpy city gent, what a country yokel, would call a Cockney.

But we got our own identity with our rhyming slang. You'll be a true Cockney if your born within the sound of Bow Bells, a church in the city of London."

Hettie stands up bows to Lena and says, "Now you are one of us. Plant your daisy roots down…,

You're an adopted Cockney.   All together,

And gawd e'lp ya'!!"

***

Meeting at St Mary and St Michael after Easter day Mass, Hettie Toke and Maggie O'Connell. Loved a good old gossip.

In between the tea, sandwiches, and home made cake, at the church social. Everyone enjoying a relaxing time after the Priest's sermon.

The Priest in his sermon, laying a bit of guilt on the Consciences of certain people.., who tried not to look guilty.

It wasn't long after the schemozzle that happened after the two lascars drowned.

"I heard it was them two from Old Sweetmans shop" said Maggie. "A right pair of dodgy feckers, so they were, I heard they were Nazi's, would you ever believe it.?"

Munching away at the food, which always was the very best. The ladies who's turn it was, took extra special care over the spread for the Priest Luncheon in the Priest Parlour.

The Parlour was big enough for a ten seater mahogany veneered extending table, ten upholstered dining chairs. There was an armchair in each side of a kitchen dresser at one end of the room. The dresser displaying a donated Alfred Meakin Indian Tree Dinner and Tea Service. A Sideboard laden with Church Pamphlets and booklets stood at the opposite end. Holy pictures adorned the walls. The floor had pine woodblock.

Putting her cup of tea, daintily down and with a very lady like dab to her mouth with a tissue.

Hettie replied

"There was so many rumours going about.

I think I believe the Police, who said they were just two laskars from off one of the ships, unloading at the docks.

The two maggots from Morry Sweetmans shop was a coincidence, or they got wind of some of the fellas coming after them, and done a disappearing act. Would you believe".

"Is it yourselves ladies? Amn'nt I the lucky one to have two of the prettiest colleens in Shadwell at my tea party. So I am."

Father Pat came up, full of a double dose of blarney.

"Whisht" Maggie laughed, "Sure you've got some guyver, so you have, Father."

"Well wouldn't you know the blarney stone and meself are made from the same yoke".

The table with half a dozen seated each side were hanging on every word and gesture from Father, a much loved Priest at St Mary and Michaels. Father Pat thrived on good natured playful baloney...,

Schmoozing, as he liked to say, if he could write a song it would be on schmoozing.

"That was a very thoughtful lesson today Father. It's a pity my lazy bunch couldn't be up to hear it."

Hettie would spend all day listening to Father Pat if she could, his easy-going affable way was so endearing. The murmur around the table and smiling agreement by all, with all eyes just waiting for Father Pat's response.

"Would you ever Hettie Toke, you'll have me blushing like one of Maggie's darling daughters, so you will."

Flapping his hand in a cheeky, saucebox way.

Father big beaming smile, looked along the table, from one to the other,

"And how's the craic?. All in the best possible taste, so..and why wouldn't it be."

He said with an exaggerated wink and a chuckle.

"I'll leave you's to your tea and cake, and bon Appetit as they say in Lallapaloosa"

Maggie and Hettie's eye's followed Father Pat glowingly.

"Mind you, getting back to them Lascars I was in Shadwell Park with my youngest, Charlie playing, and I saw a women walking down Wapping Wall towards Pelican Stairs with what looked like two Darkies, although I suppose they could have been going to the Prospect Of Whitby.." Maggie looked sideways, at Hettie...,

"The police didn't ask me, so I kept well out of it, so." Smiling Maggie added. "Sure it might not have been the day they went missing anyway."

The ladies eating the sandwiches and cakes with a smile and nod of appreciation in the direction of Mrs Lipton, the Tea lady for the day, who smiled back self importantly with a look of, I am rather clever am I not.

"I think we're well shot of them if they was Nazi's from the shop." Hettie said. "I heard they had no trousers on when they got the bodies out of the Thames. Got some funny ways about them these dago's, as my Charlie calls them"

They watched Father Pat make his benign way around his parishioners each waiting for the nod of recognition and smile.

"I see that rascal Finbarr Coen got a mention for a blessing again," Maggie spat out.

"Whish't," Hettie laughed. "Your talking about one of your own."

"That conniving gobshite. A fierce bad tempered maggot to his missus, poor Alice Maklin, and the kids…

Y'know..wears the temperance pioneer badge in his lapel as if he's taken the temperance pledge. Its only a sham.., to fool the priest's mostly.

In the pub most nights, especially Saturday up the Earl of Essex, the Irish pub on Manor Park Broadway. Because, he gets up and sings the Soldiers Song in Irish, with the band. The other boozy paddy's, think he's great would you believe."

Hettie smiled at Maggie. "Sounds like you really don't like Finn Coen."

Mrs Lipton moved along behind her satisfied and thankful tea scoffers smiling and nodding. She stopped behind Maggie. "Can I get you's ladies any more tea?, or a nice slice of soda bread and a plate of shrimps and winkles?" she raised her eyebrows questioningly and smiled wide eyed. The noise of the clinking cups and chatter of voices enjoying the craic and food,

Would go on for some time.

The ladies smiled back. Hettie thanked her but said "No that was lovely". Maggie said "Sure you did every body proud, so you have, and fair play to you." Mrs Lipton moved off, looking possibly for more praise, milk it while you can girl she thought

Maggie pulled a disgusted face, "Your one. Coen, Feckin eedjit, nasty bit of work, the kiney git.

He's a ganger man on the building site's, runs the black gang, the ground work boys.

Every Friday after work, his gang have to go with him to the nearest pub and not only buy his drink all night but give him a bung for keeping them in work.

He's got rights to higher and fire. The Bosses find it easier to let him do the business with the labourers.

He makes sure all his men are i.r.a. sympathisers. He takes the i.r.a collecting tin around the Irish pubs. Because he looks a bit fiercely strange, what with his white blond hair grey eyes, big build, always got his shirt wide open the boys call him, Paddy O'Tarzan, behind his back though. He usually gets people putting in the collecting tin, once he rattles it under their nose.

He bullies anybody if he can get away with it."

"Izzy is sort of friendly with him." Hettie whispered, with her hand in front of her face. "But my Charlie cant stand him. Charlie said he got out of being called up by saying he was doing war work. Charlie calls him a Fenian barstard. And said what happened the last time they come across Finn Coen. Would you ever know about them Fenians?" She asked Maggie.

"Aye' them bucks are the ones forever running this country down, singing about the green fields of home and how much they love their Irish home. Sure none of the feckers would ever dream of setting their great plates back, shysters and schmoozers the whole lot of erm, as Father Pat might say."

Hettie and Maggie burst in to a fit of giggling, holding hands and trying to stifle the laughter with the other hand over their mouth.

"Now now ladies, would you ever keep the noise down, do you want to see us raided by the Po..lice." Father said waving his hand down.

Father standing at the end of the dinning table couldn't help giggling along, which set the rest of the table laughing.

"Bejabbeze you terrible two, you got me banjaxed, so you have." He said face flushed holding his arms wide.

Hettie's boys were out boozing the other Saturday at a pub in Manor Park Broadway, The Earl Essex .

The pub is an imposing building of Victorian Architecture and takes up the corner on the Broadway and East Ham High Road. Entrances on each road let you into a high corniced ceiling, elegantly furnished, old fashioned stately drinking establishment, as it would have been called. The bar was dressed as you would expect any self respecting high class pub, showy, and in the best possible taste, handy which ever public, snug, saloon, or lounge bar is your class. The Band played in the lounge as it is the largest bar, and has a small dance floor in front of the stage.

Charlie, Izzy, and Connie. met a couple of old work mates, Alec Hill a site mechanic, smallish thin man, and a fella they call Big Dan Beam a short thick set man, ruddy faced. Almost the same in height and width. An apt name for a steel erector who lived like Alec local.

He was a relation of Jesse Tulip, Connie's pal. they liked a night in The Essex because the band who's in there every Saturday, they always let Izzy do a turn, and you know Izzy always game. They got settled around a table,

Facing the band. Drinks in, smoking and gossiping. Dan plonked himself in the most imposing seat, so he could have the best view.

"Izzy got the call from the Band," Hettie said "He jumps up like a banshee, with his props, as he calls them, does the long bloomer number.., have you seen that one?

Maggie said "you mean the The Old Fleesy lined? Dirty little fecker did it at the Church Social one year, nearly gave the visiting nuns a *conniption fit.*"

That set the Ladies off giggling again. "No don't start again. "Hettie said. *Putting her hand over her mouth to stop herself making to much noise, shoulders shaking instead.*

IZZY went into a couple of cockney numbers.

Boiled beef and Carrots. Just the chorus.., Boiled Beef and Carrots, Boiled Beef and Carrots,

Makes you fat and keeps you well,
That's the stuff for your darby-kel,
Don't be a vegetarian on stuff they feed to parrots,
From morn till night blow out your kite on,
Boiled beef and Carrots.

Trying his best to do a soft shoe shuffle on the cramped stage, before and after the song. He got a bit to close to the double bassist who gave him a raised arm gesture.., I'll give you a backhander in a minute, and a glare.

Charlie and the boys clapped, a few other half hearted claps came, more in sympathy.

Izzy's career as a turn had made him indifferent to applause, pubs harden the soul of performers, but they carry and on and on, until they drop, then get up and have another go. He thanked everybody most politely.

"Shall we do, After You've Gone..,? boys.."

The Band leader nodded, the double bassist, "Muttered, sooner your gone the better."

Nobody in the Earl of Essex Lounge were taking a blind bit of notice, a noisy Smokey Saturday evening boozer wise...

Af-ter You've Gone,- and Left Me Cry-ing,

Af-er You've gone,-There's no De-ny-ing,

Izzy's diction and timing got him through most songs, not quite Sinatra, but he could carry a tune.

You'll feel Blue,- You'll feel Sad,-

You'll miss the Best-est pal you've ever- had.

There'll come a time,- now don't forget it,

There'll come a time, when you'll regret it.

Oh! Babe think what your do-ing,

my love for you You know,

will drive me to ru-in,

Af-ter you've gone, after you've gone aw-ay.

Izzy stepped down from the stage, mid song and joined a couple of old soaks soft tap shuffling to the music.., a few more dancers joined them.

The atmosphere got a bit of a lift as there was entertainment to stare, or laugh at.

Either way was fine. A bit early in the evening to start any shenanigans.

Big Dan, back at the table pointed at Izzy on the dance floor, "Charlie, why does your brother have the nickname Izzy?"

"Its as plain as the nose on your face, Dan"

Charlie pulled his own nose exaggerating its length, "Touch of the yiddle about him, don't you think?"

Dan raised his eyebrows "Funny, I notice he cant talk without using his hands".

"The four be twos have come up before about us. He's the spit of our dad and granddad. We was never sure about them.

The pair of them could spin a tale or two and no mistake.

Our old man always said he should have been Mayor of Stepney, instead of that posh git Clement Atlee.

A right carve up that was.

When the Jews and Catholics joined forces to get an ordinary working person elected he was sure it would be him.

It was supposed to be between him and Morrie Sweetman, and Morrie said he would step aside and let the old man win.

From then on he'd vote for any doughnut but him, Atlee, even though he's always been a Labour man.

Like our old Grandad, he said we was related to Sir Julius Caesar as his family was all Baptised in St Dunstan's in Stepney as well." Alec who never said much exclaimed,

"Blimey O'Rielly. That's stretching it a bit… Is your old man a bit of an Eyeti as well?

Charlie laughed. "No, not the Roman. This Julius Ceasar was a Judge and MP, and a very close friend of Elizabeth the first, she spent some time staying with him in his house, so the old Grandad even suggested, with a nod and a wink…well who knows?"

Izzy meanwhile had a soppy old sod each side of him, the three of them holding hands daintily at shoulder height, trying to stay in step.

Charlie shook his head, as the boys were laughing at Izzy's nonsense.

The boozy evening chatter drifted along floating on a tide of gossip, misinformation, most of it the beer talking, not for remembering, such is beer talk, gospel at the time, shite later.

Izzy staggered back onto the stage.

He whispered to the band leader and pointed at Big Dan. The leader nodded half heartedly okay.

Izzy announced, "This one's for my old mucker. It reminds him of his missus..., who's name is Mary.

Nora Malone, call me by phone,
Number, one two three four,
Don't forget the number while you slumber,
Colleens are few,
There's none like you,
Old Erin's isle could not make me smile,
Without you Nora Malone.

Izzy stepped down from the stage as the leader called for a hand for Izzy doing a turn. The clientele had by now returned to gasbagging and forgotten all about Izzy, although he bowed graciously, thanking the none clapping boozers.

The noise of people shouting at each other had become deafening, as it by now was getting near Last Orders.

Finn Coen was waiting in front of the stage as Izzy stepped down, and grabbed the mike from Izzy's hand, roughly, pushing past him onto the stage, signalling with a raised finger and nodded cockily at the band leader, who nodded back, okay.

Finn Coen glared aggressively, mike in hand centre stage.., coughed loudly into the mike.

The pub slowly quieted down as the first few bar's of the national anthem were played, the barmen stood to attention and the boozers gradually staggered to their feet swaying, lots of coughing and groaning, and being shushed by the faithful.

At the table Connie and Alec started to rise..., looking around sheepishly. Big Dan growled, "Sit down you pratts. Its not your National Anthem." Izzy came back and stood behind Charlie, who looked over his shoulder and mouthed at him, and then Connie, with a nod, for fuck sake, sit down.

"We sing a Soldiers Song,
A Soldiers song,

With cheering rousing chorus",
Finn Coen shouted into the mike.

Staring out to see who was singing along.

Those who caught his eye would mouth nonchalantly with an innocent half a smile.

"As round our blazing fires we throng,"
Izzy sat down slowly on the side of the table by Charlie, Connie slid back down in his chair looking downcast from side to side. Alec small and wiry, managed to cross his legs under the table and become the incredible shrinking man, he took his baccy tin out of his pocket, and rolled one of the thinnest cigarettes possible, puffing away peacefully.

The five of them in an oasis of nervous silence, surrounded in a sweaty crowd of belligerent noisy singing.

Big Dan sat bolt upright. He took out of his pocket his packet of Players cigarettes and his matches with a bit of shuffling from side to side, and plonked them noisily on the table, took a cigarette out, and with a certain amount of lairyness put it to his lips, he opened the matches only to be thwarted in his lairyness because his young grandson had filled it with a leaf and a caterpillar. The boys at the table tried to stifle their laughter.

A table of four very tough looking men near the band, turned from listening attentively to Finn, and glared at the boys table with venom in their eyes.

Charlie lit Big Dans fag, who managed to hold the cigarette between his ring finger and thumb and give the vee sign with his two fore fingers.

Finn carried on, red faced and sweating in

"Sinne Fianna Fail,
Ata Faoi Gherllag Eirinn,
Buion Dar Slua,
Tha Toinn Dorainig Chugainn,
Anocht A Theimsa Bheama Baoil".

"Le gunnascreach faoi lamhach na bpilear,"
Sao libh canaigi amhean na bh fiann,

Finn raised his right arm in an all together signal, turned to the table of toughes who stood and sang, sort of in tune, a repeat of the last lines in English.

"Mid cannons roar and rifles peal,
We will chant a Soldiers Song,
A Soldiers Song."

Finn stood to attention head bowed while the band finished.

A Smokey atmospheric silence descended on the pub.

The table of toughs stood to attention and did the sign of the cross.

Daffy the cross terrier dog, another regular of the pub sat, in front of the them charmingly paws up in his best begging pose. Skedaddled smartly when a boot was angrily kicked at him.

The pub stayed silent until Finn raised his head and clapped.

The pub went back to its normal shouting, Smokey, sweaty, glass clanking Saturday night,

Hullabaloo.

A Priest sitting a the back in a corner with friends, came up to Finn, shook his hand, and had a quick word. They both looked over at toughs, the Priest raised a finger, nodding, in easy boys.., admonishment. Finn still holding Fathers handshake, said "No worries Father.., goodnight. "The Priest made his way out of the pub, raising his hand looking around and smiling, the regulars, who called back,.. see you Father.

Finn made his way to the boys table, stopping at the toughs table for a word. He acknowledge the calls of, fair play, good on 'yer boyo, nice one Finn.

Coming up behind Izzy, eyeballing Dan.., who glared back.., then looking around at the others one by one, Dan never took his eyes of Finn.

"Is it yourself Izzy.., enjoying the craic,..so." He said with his thin wavy frog lipped snarl.

Izzy tilting his head back.

"Finbarr.., how yer doing? Your in fine voice, still got it I see.., always could carry a tune., so you can. Still got the Irish'. so"

"Aye.., I can still give it the bigun if I need to.

The boys over yonder," he jerked his thumb at the toughs. "Expect the Irish song, when they turn up."

"We were all having a giggle at Dan who was going to light his fag with his grandsons pet, a caterpillar, that was in Dans matchbox."

Dan explained that if young Ken, or Bobsy, as Dan affectionately called him, was playing with the matches he'd likely get a skelp from his Mother. The boys laughed nervously.

Finn looked sternly around the group settled his eyes back on Dan. "Very funny..," he said sneeringly.

"Is that right your working on the flats at Stepney Way?" Izzy asked.

"Sure I am, how dyou know? "Finn snapped.

"You've lived long enough in the East End, Finbarr to know we all know whats what."

Finn laughed.

"Aint that a fact. If it's a job your after Izzy, you'll need a big shovel to work in me gang. Hard graft in the black gang, so it is."

Meanwhile Dan reached across the table with a questioning eye at Connie's packet of Smiths crisps, who nodded back okay. Dan gingerly opened the crisps and folded the sides flat.

The boys plus Finn, who was talking, followed Dans every move, with the crisps spread evenly on the opened packet Dan gave a whistle, as he bent and place the packet on the floor by his feet, Daffy the black and white mongrel dog came scooting up to make a crispy crunching noisy snack of Dans generosity, who called over to a barman for a clean ashtray, so he could fill it full of beer to quench Daffy's thirst, who slurped greedily.

Connie asked Dan if he called the dog Daffy, Dan nodded. When told his full name is Daffodil. Connie laughed." What a silly name for a dog."

"No not really.., not when the poor dog owners known as Wally the Welk" replied Dan.

Finn said dismissively. "I'll wish yous goodnight, mind how go." The boys were pleased to see him go.

He lumbered back to the toughs table, said something and nodded backwards at the boys table. The toughs glanced over at the boys, then noisily joined the rest of the general hubbub as the, last orders, was shouted by the bar staff.

"That Finn is talking to them Pikey's,"

Alec said. "Don't look round… "naturally they did.

"That's them pikey's that caused the big ruck in the Blackesly the other month."

"Don't worry Al, we're all behind you." said Dan. "That Finn.., as my old Irish Granny would say.., That maggot, he's a fekkin gobshite."

As they all rose to go home the noise of scrapping chairs, customers shouting goodnight coughing some cursing.

Charlie manoeuvred his way up slowly, signalled to his son and brother to get up.

He smiled around the boys.

"We've had a fair old night.., right."

They jostled their way outside happy in their cups, as the posh'es say. Enjoying fresh air wafting over from the Wanstead Flats, as that part of Epping forest was called.

"Bus coming," yelled Connie as him and his Father and Uncle, ran to catch the no 25 to take them back to Stepney Green.

"You two be allright" Charlie shouted back at Dan and Alec.

As the boys waited at the bus stop, Dan drew a foot long shaped iron tool from his belt, shouting back across the road.

"I've got my trusty Podger, we'll have no bother." Alec and Dan laughing and jostling, waived goodnight.

"What the bleeding hell's he got there?" Izzy asked.

"Don't know much do you Izzy..?that is a Podger you use on a SGB scaffolding clip."

Connie, at last able to get a word in.

"Smart arse little git aintcha." Izzy shouted back…

Hettie mentioned in passing that that Finn bloke yelled out to her as she was passing the new flats at Stepney Way. Had the cheek to say he was drinking with my boys a few weeks ago.

Hettie linked her arm with Maggie as they made their way out of an enjoyable care free feast without the bother of having to clear up dirty dish's. Bosum friends forever.

Finn Coen's first ruck of the day was stamping into the Black gangs hut and shifting his surly lot out and grafting. He would glare at them daring one of them to have a moan. He pursed his thin lips hoping to get his day away with a fierce shouting insulting ruck at any gobshite.

The noise of a building site with mobile generators, concrete mixers, dumper trucks, and always someone with a big hammer knocking hell out of a piece of metal, early morning, didn't drown Finn Coen's great gob.

As the other workers moved about site, chuckling to each other giving a nod at the black gangs hut, "He's at it already, Paddy McGinty's goat, what a twat." The chippy's pointed with their thumb.

Finn and his Black Gang were digging out the earth and rubble between the Steel Piles that had been hammered down by the Pile Driving Crane, making a channel fourteen foot apart.

The Steel Piles were braced apart by foot square thick timber joists resting on steel brackets welded onto the piles. The bracing timbers were set twelve foot intervals.

A crane at the top of the diggings would lower its earthmoving bucket under the directions of Finn, who did the Banksman's job himself, so knew the hand and finger signals for the crane driver to control the earth moving bucket. Down at the bottom of the diggings, him and his gang would tidy up the earth stuck against the Piles that the earthmover couldn't reach. The black gang would keep digging until the Site Agent told them to stop, if he dropped dead gawd knows where they'd end up.

Busy working away they heard a shout from above, looking up the Site Agent's runner, Winston, was bellowing at them standing by the access ladder.

"Hey.., Hey.., which one of you., is Peter Mac?"

Peter raised his hand tentatively then dropped it when Finn, Yelled up,

"Who wants to know." With the noise from the Crane, it took a fair amount of hollering to be heard. Winston leaning over the tethered top of the ladder shouted.

"Mister Struthers told me to get Peter Mac to empty the Piss buckets on the landings in the Main building, they're getting busy now the second fixing have started."

His aggressive pointing and hand waving provoked Finn no end.

"Tell Mister Struthers we're to busy.., so you can empty the piss buckets yourself.., you shitehawk,"

Winston turns his back and wiggles his backside, at Finn taking the mickey while singing.. diddle diddle.. diddle di do diddly de and doing a jig. As he walked away, Sending Finn into a conniption fit.

"I'll stick your head in a piss bucket if I come up there, so I will.."

"Turn it up Finn me old mucker," Peter Mac piped up." He gets me bets on, he's not only the Site Agents runner, he's the bookies runner.., on the side, a bit fly is yon Winston wouldn't you know."

Peter Mac always looked like a bundle of rags, small stature, but a grafter, and willing for any work, betting as necessary as breathing.

"Peter.., get on wid'dyour work, take no notice of the blackie. I'll go and see Ivor Struthers me 'self."

The ladder was trembling under Finn's stamping on his way out of the diggings. His march across the building site around mixers, piles of bricks, scaffolding and every type of yoke.., didn't, although he never stopped muttering to himself, once trip up, even wearing Wellington boots, tops folded over, of course, so used to a building site, was himself...

Izzy on his nights around the music pubs, hoping he'd be asked to do a turn, found it a bit strange how Finbarr Coen seemed to turn up, time and again. Its true the same old star struck show offs put themselves on offer, all mad as a box of frogs, Izzy and Finn included.

The Toke Family enjoying a night out, Hettie, Charley, Izzy, Connie, and Lena, at The Watermans Arms. Dockside. East London.

Well known for entertainment in the best possible taste, plenty of risqué double-entendres by the compere in a boozy pub'y style, just the way the Cockney Luv's like it.

The Family had managed to squeeze themselves in on a long table, and with drinks in

were chatting away nonchalantly half expecting Izzy to get the nod to do a turn.

Izzy studiously looked everywhere but at the stage while craftily keeping his eye's on the pub mirrors reflecting the band. Hopefully getting the call, going into the act of being surprised, not sure if he should, until coerced by the compere, and reluctantly, with the roar of the crowd in his ears, well his family mostly, he'd apologetically with a shy smile pick his prop bag up and make his way slowly to the stage. A noisy singalong with the entertainer.

Mrs Shufflewick was giving her version of ;

Daddy Wouldn't Buy Me A Bow Wow,
Daddy Wouldn't Buy Me A Bow Wow,
I've Got A Little Cat And I'm Very Fond Of That,
But I'd Rather Have A Bow Wow Wow,
A Great Dane Type Bow Wow Wow,
Ah girls? I don't mind if I do, he said with a leering wink.

Izzy his mind elsewhere hadn't heard Finn Coen come up behind him and was singing along with the family.

"You following me about Izzy?"

"Oh its yourself Finn.., bleed'n., hell you gave me a turn creeping up like that.. You know the family don't you". As he pointed with his index finger and swept it around the family.

Finn Coen smart suit and loosened tie casually smiled to everybody. A short back and sides haircut, with quiff, Bryll-creamed to darken his white hair a bit back to the blond hair he was so proud off. Alice the missus said he was the spit of Burt Lancaster, the film star, looks and stamp. She was a tad overwhelmed.

"Charley., how you doing?"

Who nodded back.

A big beaming smile for Hettie.

"Mrs Toke your looking well, enjoying yourself?.. Can I get you all a drink?"

"We're all okay Finn.., thanks" Said Izzy.

Finn turned his beaming smile on Lena.

"So Connie.., this is the grand bonnie lass I heard about.., is it not?" He chuckled.

Lena and Connie gave a friendly nod back.

"The job's still open on the shovel."

He said to Izzy laughing.

"Are you joking Finn for gawd sake. One has one's act to polish.., don't you know. Us theatricals are at it none stop. One is expecting a call any moment." Izzy's Sunday accent was very posh.

Finn looked from Charlie to Hettie.

"There's a job on site for some one to run the canteen, coming up," he looked quizzically at Hettie eyebrows raised, then eyeballed Charlie. "Be a good little earner for someone handy. I'd get Alice to do it but you know what she's like, away with the fairy's half the time. That why she never does the priest tea days.

The site agent will pay for the canteen to be set up. and then give the person running it a float. He's getting fed up with the boys sloping off site to get a sandwich."

Hettie and Charlie looked at each other questioningly eye's raised. Charlie shrugged his shoulders in a down to you attitude, at Hettie.

The drummer gave a drum roll for a bit of hush.

The noisy smoky glass clanking atmosphere slowly diminished half-heartedly.

Mrs Shufflewick drag artiste impersonator fag in one hand and drink in the other, makeup as a frumpy old tart, red beret on the back of the head, the remains of a good time girl…? but a jolly good all round chap. Looked over at Izzy and gave him the eyes nodding a silent yes?

Izzy slowly rose and shrugged a shake of his head and.., a if I must grin. Never with out his carrier bag of props he gently wormed his way through the packed boozers.

"Now ladies and gentlemen and others, from entertaining Royalty he's come straight to us from the Queens Arms, and we all know what queen..", he said with a leery wink. "And the Kings Head.." And a leery wink, with the other eye. Izzy stepped up on the stage to a drum roll

And cymbal roll.

"Its your friend and mine. Jim., Izzy., Toke.

We can offer you the first exposure, of a touch of class, if there's any hintellectuals here.., pin back your lugholes." Finn put two hands on the back of Izzy's vacant chair, smiled at Charlie, nodded down, "D'you mind if join you?" Charlie raised a hand and okayed. Finn sat and applauded loudly with the family, and whistled fingers in mouth and laughing loudly.

The drummer gave another drum and cymbal roll.., Mrs Shufflewick waved a finger of annoyance and glared at him, so he did another drum roll only longer, just as Mrs Shufflewick went to speak the drummer did a taradiddle on the cymbals. Mrs Shufflewick took a deep breath, anger on her face, looked round at the drummer, then back at the audience, rolled her sleeves up exaggeratedly

Turned around, strode back to the drummer, who sheepishly grinned, snatched the drumsticks out of his hands and threatened to stick them up his nose.

Going back to the mike.

"Now as I was saying before I was rudely interfered with..," You should be so lucky".one of the audience shouted.

"And you can shut your cakehole.."she shouted at a laughing punter, who shouted back," Get on with it for gawdsake."

The noise in the pub was building so Mrs Shufflewick had a word with Izzy, nodded at the pianist, who mouthed back, Right.

"We will now do a duet for one, of that well known Aria..,
O Mio Babbino Caro, I will sing in a high contralto and my
assistant, will help me reach the F sharp, with the aid of a drum
stick."

Passing a drum sticks to Izzy who theatrically

Jabbed the sticks up and down with a pained expression on
his face. Mrs Shufflewick made an eyes raised grimace face at
Izzy. Turned to the pianist.

"Professor after three…" Coughing delicately into his hand.

O Mio Babbino Caro..,

O My Beloved Father..,

What A Right Misery Guts Was He..,

Our Beloved Mama used as a skivvy was she..,

She went to uncle's to buy her own wedding ring..,

Pigeons And Paddy The Dog, The only Pals For Fagin..,

Andrei Sul Shadwell Docks..,

Ma Per Buttarmi in Thames..,

Mi Struggo E Mi Tormento..,

Babbo Pieta Babbo Pieta..,

Babbo Pieta Babbo pieta.

Izzy coming from behind Mrs Shufflewick as she attempted
the high note, for a big finish, and curtsying, to some clapping
and laughter. Izzy produced from his props the long bloomers
he used in one of his acts hung them on the drum sticks waving
them around, to a big a big cheer.

"Oi she shouted d'you mind, they're clean on this month."

The saucy punter shouted "lorst your drawers again, you old
tart"

"Have you still got last months pretty pink ones." She
answered back shyly.

During the song Lena and Hettie sang together in Italian,
along with the performers, quietly, and, more in tune than the
act.

The pub increased in noise with the customers able to get back to what they were there for, shouting drinking laughing.

Finn watched the two ladies, he couldn't hear them because of the general noise of a pub at full throttle on an entertainment night, but vaguely caught they were singing in a foreign language.

"Were you singing that song in German? He asked, impressed.

Lena shook her head, then looked at Hettie, who said "Italian., it's a well known aria in Germany though." They both giggled.

Mrs Shufflewick back on the mike. "We got to let Izzy do a turn.., after all the help he gave me.., one way and another.., aint we..?"

"As long as long as he don't wave another pair of your Kecks about". Saucy punter laughing yelled.

"There aint no more, you should know, you kept last months ones." Mrs Shufflewick said, and gave a shy glance and flick of the wrist.

The crowd around the heckler gave him a right shy, ikeing, laughing and pushing him, for trying it on with a put down artiste, what a Wally.

Mrs Shufflewick coughed into the mike and *announced*

"Keeping the Farvers songs going. Izzy will now do..," He turned to Izzy who took the mike.

"I'm Following in Farvers Footsteps…
To Fol-low In Your Far-vers Foot-Steps,
Is a Mo-tto For Each Boy..,
And Fo-lowing In Far-vers Foot-steps,
Is A Fing, I Much En-joy..,
Me Muvver Caught Me Out One Night,
Up The West End On A Spree..,
She Said Oi What You Doing?,
And I Answered Don't Ask Me..,

I'm Fo-lowing In Far-vers Foot-steps,
I'm Fol-owing Me Dear Old Dad,
He's Just In Front Wiv A Fine Big Gal,
So I Thought I Would Have One As Well..,
I Don't Know Where He's Going..,
But When He Gets There I'll Be Glad,
I'm Fo-lowing In Farvers Foot-steps,
YES!,
I'm Fo-lowing Me Dear Old Dad.

Mrs Shufflewick meanwhile was doing a soft shoe shuffle.

For a Curry up in Pennyfields Last night I Went,
And Pa Went There As Well.,
How Many Lem-on-ades we Had my Word I Really Could-nt Tell,
At Two A m Pa Started Orf For Home Brahms And Listz And So Did I..,
Folks Said, Mind Where Your Go-ing, But I Simply Made Reply..,
I'm Fo-llowing in Farvers Foot-steps,
I'm Fo-lowing me dear Old Dad.
He's Wobb-ling On In Front You See,
And Pon My Word He's Worse Than Me,
I Don't Know Where He, s Going But,
When He Gets There I'll Be Glad..,

Izzy and Mrs Shufflewick sang together at the mike,

I'm Fo-llowing In Farvers Foo-steps.., YES..,
We're Fol-owing Our Dear Old D-ad...

Then the pair did a soft shoe shuffle knees up, curtsied to each other and hugged laughing. Izzy's family and others sporadically clapped, Finn smiling all around to each one of the family clapping and smiling.., shouting, "Good on you Izzy".

Mrs Shufflewick patted Izzy on the back as he stepped down from the stage. She announced,

"Now all the way from Irish town, Wapping., that broth of a boy.., Finn Coen.., get up Finn."

Finn wasn't one to be coy, he was up like a shot. As he passed Izzy they shook hands and a friendly pat on the shoulder. Izzy sat back on the seat with the family .they all congratulated him on a good job.

Lena leant over the table smiling and squeezed his hand. The smoky noisy atmosphere was reaching a crescendo of ear-splitting throat choking level. Charlie lip synced to Hettie, 'have you had enough' Hettie caught Lena and Connie's eye with a questioning nod towards the door, receiving an affirmative.

Charlie told Izzy, who was in the middle of lighting a well earned smoke.

"We're gonna shoot.., you coming?"

"I'm gonna hang on for a while." All the conversation done with hand signals, and lip sync .

"Tell Finn we'll come up to the site Monday morning, about that canteen job."

The family got up to leave as Finn started singing, squeezed through the crowd catching the first catchy words of Hank Williams song,

"Hey Good Looking Watcha Got Cookin,"

Finn's eye's following Hettie.., when she looked back at him.., he winked and waved. His flamboyant lairyness was eyeballing any middle age crumpet, given half a chance..?

"How's About Cooking Something Up With Me,"

As they emerged from the all embracing pub cosiness, into chilly Dockside East End, they caught Finn's last bit of the song.

"Hey Sweet Baby Don't You Think Maybe,"

Charlie, Hettie, Connie out of tune, and Lena, sang, as they walked back home.

"We could Find Us A Brand New Recipe,
I Got A Hot Rod Ford...,

So If You Wanna Have Fun..,"

You got that wrong Dad.

No its not.

That put the kybosh on the song, and they all started giggling.

Strolling home in Dockland after a great night in a pub might be a bit daunting for some but if your born and bred locally you belong, no where else, Charlie despite his hardships thought like the little book said 'These My Brethren'. He felt good and happy in his Manor. The Plague. didn't shift us. The Great Fire of London didn't shift us. The Nazi's didn't shift us, The Slum Clearance mob are doing their best to shift us, can we resist them? Cause we can, even if the Black Plague descends on us again. Cockney till I die, as my Brethren would say.

"Come on Charlie.., all together" Hettie said.

Linking arms with Lena and Connie, Charlie walking in front, they attempted to sing.

"Hey Good Looking, Wotcha Got Cooking".

Sitting in Mr Struthers office in the Stepney way building site. Hettie and Charlie were being given all the particulars of the proposed new canteen and her job details.

"It's a pleasure to meet you Mr and Mrs Toke.

Finn.., I believe explained about the Canteen Manageress's job?" They both nodded.

A tap on the door brought Finn opening the door and poking his smiling face in.

"Come in Finn" Mr Struther said,

"Take a seat while I tell these good people the details and Job description, and most of all the wages..," He said, with a smile. The canteen was on the left as you came in the gates. its being fitted out at the moment? "He looked at Finn who nodded yes." You will have your own door, that leads you into the cooking area, there will be the counter and a door will lead out to the seating area. The kitchen has the usual utensils and worktop, fridge and larder, a small gas hob will be fitted, for frying, but we will wait to see if its needed. I will order a tray of rolls and a couple of loafs from a local bakery and ham cheese eggs, from a wholesaler and what ever you get asked for tea and milk, of course. Can you come in Friday

And get everything ship shape and ready for Monday.?"

Hettie said "Yes I'll look forward to it."

"If you start off working as normal, Your hours would be Nine o'clock till three thirty. If you find you need help.., we could get you help on a casual basis. Cash in hand, You will be staff, so I can pay you the tradesman rates. Now Mrs Toke would the Job and wages suit?",

Mr Struthers smiled warmly at Hettie.

She looked at Charlie questioningly.., Charlie shrugged in a sort of, yes, I suppose so.

Mr Struthers rose shook hands with Hettie and Charlie.

"It's a pleasure to meet you both. My door is always open, Mrs Toke, a well fed site is a happy team, so you will be very important to me, you just tell me any thing you want to run an efficient canteen and I'll fix it.

Finn, show Mrs Toke around the new canteen.

I'll see you Friday, Mrs Toke".

Finn said "Right you are Mr Struthers."

Finn held the door open and the three of them went across the site entrance, opposite the site engineers offices and cabins, to Hettie's canteen.

Just as they walked warily across the entrance avoiding the usual muddiness of a site, the madman with the big hammer started knocking belloil out of a concrete mixing drum, the noise carrying up to the Festival Hall and could easily be part of The Anvil Chorus on Verdi's Il Travatore. The general noise made Hettie put her hands over her ears until they got into the canteen.

Folding tables and forms for seating stacked along one side.

"Me.. self and a couple of my boyo's will get these sorted out before you come in on Friday,

So don't worry. He's one of the best, so he is.., Mr Struthers. I reckon you'll need help so I do, If you have a friend..? who could do with a few bob. As you probably noticed I'm Mr Struther's

Right hand man, his general Pooh Bah, as they say." Finn had overheard one of the engineers talking to Mr Struthers about him and thought it must good, so he quite liked the sound of being a Pooh Bah.

"Finn," Charlie said, "I'll get you a drink for rowing Hettie in here, you've done us a right favour."

"Whisht, Sure it's a pleasure, keeping the jobs local. But I'm partial to a ball of malt.., drop of the Jameson, or Colne Valley Barley Wine goes down a treat wouldn't you know.., I must get back to my bunch of toerags now, got to get the pile driving going. You'll feel some thumping from it, and noise, don't worry its only intermittent, you'll soon get used to the noises of a building site in full swing. So if you wont mind I'll say tat tar.., and I'll see you Friday Hettie". He said with a wink.., and nodded at Charlie.

As they made their way off site stamping on the pavement to get rid of some mud on their shoe's the fact that their home was minutes away in Jubilee Street made the job very acceptable.

"Do you remember when Connie, the little rascal hid in the bombed debris here, it took all the neighbours and a couple of cops, hours, until one of his mates led us to the little toerags den hidden in the cellar of one of the bombed houses. "Said Hettie.

Hettie and Charlie chatting on the way back from the canteen job. Walking along Stepney Way, the noise in East London from the docks, building sites and traffic made Charlie's hope for a regeneration of his beloved manor, a new cockney life as it once was.., in his dreams..

Charlie raising his voice slightly.

"Blimey Gel we've seen some bleeding bomb sites, makes you think if there's any more disasters us cockney's have got to put up with."

"I know Charlie., all the trauma of us going through Germany in their blitz, then coming back to the devastation here. The awful loss to the pair of us. Your Doreen getting killed early on in the bombing. God knows what happened to my Parents..?"

As they turned into Jubilee Street they stopped to look up and down the street.., and dwell for a moment.

"Still Charlie, we haven't done too badly considering… I've tried to do the best by you, a companion to you and a Mother to Connie."

"Gel you've been my old Dutch.., as the old song says, you've done us proud.., cockney through and through, and I'm well pleased. As a Mother to Connie.., Doreen would be thankful, I'm sure."

Charlie looked at Hettie smiling wistfully, a sideways nod of.., your alright Gel.., affection.

On Friday Hettie opened the site canteen door and found the tables and seats all organized.

Finn sitting at one of the tables lounging with his legs stretched out along the form seating.

"Top of the morning Hettie, fine morning, so it is. How you do in?"

"I'm fine Finn thanks." A smiling Hettie said.

"I've got everything fixed.., me darlin. Just needs yourself to get familiar with your work area. If you make sure, the gas hob, and all the electrical stuff works. I'll show you where all the pots and pans cutlery and dish cloths are. You move things about to suit yourself, your in charge in here. Get used to being the Boss.., sounds good ah, the big Boss.." Finn laughed, Hettie joined in. He opened the serving hatch while Hettie busied herself in the kitchen opening cupboard doors and draws. "Its kind of you to take time out from you own work, you sure you wont get into trouble?"

"No., No., No., don't worry, Mr Struthers said to spend as much time as possible to get you up and running. He's keen you make a go of the canteen. Besides he was going to give you Winston for the day. That's

His gofer, his runner."

"Gofer? Runner..? Hettie chuckled. Finn laughed.

"You never heard that before?, you know, gofer this gofer that. He's a darkie, too bleeding fly by half, next to useless, a bodger and a half. Besides.., my piling crane is out of action for the day, so I said I'd get you started. As we're friends he expects me to help you in anyway possible. Parishioners of St Mary and Michaels pray together, work together, what could be cosier." He said conspiratorially.

"I'm sure Father Pat would approve of good pals. Thanks again Finn you've been a treasure. The wages will be a big help as my Charlie only gets a few days a week at the Free Trade Wharf These days, because of the asthma, not in the best of health, poor Charlie, bless him."

"Sure haven't the Irish and the Germans always been the best of friends, before the war and after, our President the great Eamon De Valera was even upset when Hitler died. Mind you.., Despite being a Yank we still think of him as a kosher Paddy.

Your from Germany aren't you.?" He asked.

Hettie shook her head vehemently "Not now Finn. I'm an adopted cockney. Gawd 'elp me." And got a fit of the giggles, thinking what a Kinney git. Finn smiled at Hettie's laughter.

"Charlie should do what I do. I never get sick."

He stood tall flexing his shoulders and generally swanking about, blue donkey jacket, muddied, crumpled shirt half done up, baggy old trousers, thick leather belt, wellington boots turned over at the top, the very model of a major ganger man.

Hettie thought, keep smiling Gel, let him carry on carrying on.

"Even if I did get sick I wouldn't trust one of them posh gits, haven't forgiven the Labour Party for nationalising the health service, they got no time for working men. No.., the Irish Black Doctors the Kiddee, you can always trust the Cure from them Boyos."

"You mean you go back to Ireland if you do get sick,"

"No.., no.., me darling, we're much more sophisticated.., what you do is wrap a five pound note around a lock of hair and I post it to my cousins who live near Letterkenny, not far from where the magic Black Doctors place.., in the foothills of Muckish Mountain, Upper Dunmore, Dun, Na, Ngal, just a hamlet really. His cottage is the oldest there, outside lavee, St Patricks Well in the yard for his water.., local people swear by it for their health. He looks like a little pixie, he says the well waters for drinking not washing."

"I come from a small village, but I don't remember much about it, but I have heard of faith healers." Hettie looking interested.

"What exactly does he do,?" She asked.

"Well.., he says a blessing on the hair holding it in his hand.., like he does if your there in person, laying the hands on. If you want an extra special blessing.., for few pounds more he takes it down to the Fairey Grotto at the bottom of his yard. Its a bit of scrub land with some old hawthorn bush's and weeds about ten foot in the round, it sits between gardens and yards, the locals never go near it.., a place where only himself and the little people go at night.., some say they've seen phantoms in the grotto, illusionism's an the like, cause they turn the eyes away and cross themselves.., don't look to see too much, it might be himself, but then again too phantasmagorical. Sure I don't altogether believe in the unknown meself, still you can never be too careful. For extra extra special people.., he'll pick a bit of fairy hair caught on the hawthorn bush and send it back with your own hair, or if your there give it to you…All you do for the Cure is hold it on the offending part as long as you can between sundown and sunrise.., and shazam.., job done.., cured." Finn plonked himself down at one of the tables laughing." Now I'm not telling porkies it's the god's honest truth.., so it is."

"I believe you, thousands wouldn't." Hettie giggled.

"The missus swears by him, sure over the years she's had a lot of the old woman's problems' so if you get any of those you can always have a word with herself, so you can., Not that you're an old women, me darling. No.., No.., you'd be a fine figure of women so you would."

He smiled ingratiatingly.

Hettie smiled enigmatically. "Thanks Finn.., your to kind."

Her self control stopped her from collapsing with laughter, or god forbid wetting herself.

"Finn Coen you are a caution, and no mistake, talk about the gift of the gab," Hettie at last could let the giggling have free rein.

"Sure we need a good old laugh. I can be a bit of a devil, when I like. For a lark I made an imitation bomb and threw it over the wall of the Mint at Tower Hill. I got a cardboard box from work, packed it with fireworks, someone told me to put a box of Swan Vester match's with a large wireless battery and if I wire the terminals together, it would heat up, set the match's alight and set off the fireworks. I lugged it all the way up Cable Street lobbed it over the wall.

I legged it to the Tower and sat on the bench's there. Nothing happened, apart from me looking a right dork.

It was reported as a major incident. Police, Fire Brigade the lot"

He laughed till he nearly had a conniption fit, tears in his eyes.

"Will I make a brew you Finn, the tea and sugar things are in the larder, no milk though." Hettie offered.

He looked at his watch. "No darling, a caw fee when I get back, hen, that's fine, I take it black, three sugars.., got to keep my sweetness up."

He said with a wink, and a slyly mocking smile.

"I must see to my boy's. Will you be alright on your own for a while.?"

Hettie nodded.

Finn smiled and went out of the canteen slamming the door.

Hettie sat down at a table taking a deep breath, drifting into her thought's. The noise of the site diminishing in the entirety of her day dreams.

(Momma darling.., this is a strange man. Have you ever heard the like of him..? he doesn't stop swanking. Mutti… Sorry I'm not thinking.., you wont know what that means.., I know your giggling, I love to hear your lovely chuckle. He's so full of himself. But he's helped us with this job so I mustn't be unkind.) 'Good for you, sweetie, I don't want to see you getting hard hearted, Sube.., the thing with the other two dark men, is in the past, and forgotten'. (Danke schone, Mutti.)

A tap on the door and it suddenly opening, brought Hettie back to reality. Maggie O'Connell seeing Hettie stepped inside.

"There you are, is it alright.?"

"Yes., Yes, come inside, Maggie, glad to see you, so I am."

They both laughed at Hettie's Irishism.

"He wont be long. I can't make you a cup of tea, we haven't any milk, unless you want a cuppa without?"

Maggie screwed her face up, shaking her head. They were just about to have a good gossip, when the door burst open and Finn barged in.

He looked a bit surprised." Ah its your self Missus is it."

Maggie, a sixty something formidable no nonsense lady, salt of the earth, Finn was a bit cowed down in her presence, one of the few people in the world, who looked right through him, and knew all the dirty strokes he'd got up to.., and giving him the eye.., told him. About five foot three of aggravation, in his eye's. Dressed in a pair of booties, dark blue skirt, a pinnie over that, a long thick cardie and a beret on her head.

She sat down next to Hettie who explained.

"You know you said get another pair of hands..? Maggie's agreed to help out. D'you think that will be alright?"

Sitting down opposite the ladies. Finn put his hand up to his chin thinking.

"Mister Struthers, left this canteen Malarkey in my hands so I don't see why not. You know its cash in hand Mrs?" Maggie nodded. "I can leave everything in Hettie hands then."

They all had a friendly group smile.

"Now the new canteen manager might christen the joint by making us all a nice cup of caw fee, thee lumps for me, I don't mind if I do, tar very much." All eyes on Finn. He strode up and down in the middle of the canteen. Centre of attention, just the way he liked it.

"You know thinking of it, you might be just the right two for the job.

With Maggie O'Connell to keep any saucy nonsense, from the boys in check. And I'm sure she can…" He looked at Maggie questionaly.

She gave him a slight nod of the head, in a, have no doubt about that and smiled at Hettie, who nodded enthusiastically .

"With what you Ladies coped with during the war, looking after your family, managing to get them fed and safe. Sure managing a bunch of hairy arsed builders will be a piece of cake, if you pardon my French."

The Ladies went into the kitchen to make the coffee's leaving Finn to stretch himself out along a form opposite the table bearing the Ladies shopping bags. With the chatter from the kitchen. Finn smiled to himself thinking he could be on a stone bonk winner here.., am'ent I the clever little fecker.

"Isn't this just grand. All of us from St Mary and Michaels, so we should get on fine, especially with Father Pat not five minutes away."

Finn feeling on top of the world as he felt the Ladies would be a good sauce of gossip of any shenanigans, or plots, in any finer feelings paranoid, is always there, but with these two Ladies watching my arse.

Cosy with the Irish chit chat about this that and them, the odd bit of gossip and scandal about this one or that one. They giggled and chuckled away and let Finn tell his other bit of fun.., as he called it.

"I was telling Hettie a couple of tales about a lark I got up to get the old busies running around." He looked at Maggie. Laughing

"You'll enjoy this bit of business, so you will. One up for the boys. I did an imitation bomb and chucked it in the Mint. A couple of weeks later I did a better one, I found an old rusty gas bottle on the rubbish dump

On a building site down by the docks where I was working a few weeks back, I tied an old alarm clock to the top, wrapped

it in a sack, walked over Tower Bridge and dropped it right in the middle where the Bridge split in to two." He was laughing fit to burst looking from one Lady to the other, who smiled most politely. The

female expression of what a complete buck eedjit shone in both pair of eyes.

"I slowly strolled across and turned left down Tooley Street and into a pub and had my usual, a Barley Wine and a double Irish, when I came out, the traffic was backed up from Tower Bridge in all directions, I had to walk to Rotherhithe Tunnel and get a bus through to Wapping. That was a great craic, so it was.

Them Boyo's, that was in the Earl Of Essex when I saw your family.., Hettie.., the other week.., to be honest them boyos thought your family was taking the piss..,, pardon my French. I had to have a word with them, told them Charlie was a pal of mine…Well, this is the best bit .., They give me some dough, they thought I was being patriotic, said it came from the top boys of the IRA."

Finn was convulsed with laughter slapping his thighs.

"What d'you think of that Missus wasn't that the niftiest joke ever."

Maggie gave him a look of.., Jesus what a load of old Twaddle.., this man is asking for trouble from those gobshite's from the I.R.A.

Thinking he'd get some sort of admiring response from Maggie he concentrated on her, being Irish.., little realizing Maggie had been in dockside East London, left there, with her sister from the age of eleven, her sister being thirteen. All of her eight children being brought up to be proud to be English, she herself being proud to bring them up as English, and her children, immensely proud of a loving Irish Mother.

Seeing Maggie didn't seem that impressed. He tried to make more jokes.

"just a bit of fun Mrs, you know what us Irish are like, full of the old blarney."

A smiling Hettie thought, this man is worse than people think, he's a right stinker, despite amiableness. Her Mothers comments about not being too judgemental darling.., you don't know his history sweetie…

Hettie placid by nature would always rebel if her cockney Brethren were threatened in any way.

"Finbarr Coen you're a mean man so you are.., Waffle.., Twaddle., Jesus.., your full of the old blarney."

Maggie had just finished talking when the roar of an engine starting up made her jump nearly spilling her coffee, she held her cup in two hands any way because of a slight shake. Suddenly a loud thump and a slight earth tremor at their feet made the Ladies spill their coffee. Finn laughed with a swagger of his shoulders.

"Don't worry girls, that's just my pile driver. The mechanic said he might get it going this afternoon. You'll soon get used to it. Now I'll have to get back to the diggings.., Ladies. Will you be up for it on Monday morning?" He smiled ingratiatingly.

The ladies chorused "Yes thank you Finn."

He clumped towards the door as he opened it he shouted over his shoulder, "I'll be here to open up for the delivery's so everything will be cushty.., bye.., bye."

Maggie and Hettie sat sipping their coffee.., what was left of it. Staring at the still trembling slammed door, Finn's presence and aura still inhabiting.

"Bejabbers..," Maggie exclaimed. "Would you ever look at the height and size of it.., What a maschigena.., What have we let our selves in for,,? Yon eedyit is not the full turn of the coin, so he's not."

Hettie giggled, "Maschigena the right word for himself.., so it is."

They started laughing fit to burst with a few Girlie shrieks and tears in the eyes.

Once the canteen was up and running after only a few weeks, Maggie and Hettie had organized the food and drinks to most tastes, any moans were delt with by Maggie, bringing eight children up with a politically minded docker for a Husband, she was capable of dealing with any stroppy disgruntled site worker. Hettie made of the same mettle as Maggie but with a more mild intelligence. The two Ladies made the canteen a pleasant home from home for the hairy arsed worker navvies. The boys soon learnt how far to go with the banter and saucy remarks, any jack the lads trying it on with Hettie, got the rough end of Maggie's tongue, and she could hold her own in any competition in the docks for swearing. The fellas soon treated the Ladies like their own Family, any bad language was frowned on in the Ladies presence, as it is in general in the Dockside homes, respect for Mother is expected, if not forthcoming.., a smack around the back of the head usually produces respect. With a touch of the Mary Whitehouse zealotry, Maggie censored the fellas reading. Any mucky magazines were banned, like Parade, or Spick or Span, anybody caught, got the old lady evil all-knowing eye, and the ridiculing "You dirrr., tty little Fecker." To loud and laughing abuse, from the boys, for the rest of the day. Jesse Tulip got a couple of days working on site, welding brackets on the steel piling to hold the bracing timbers. Being a bit of lairey cockney no one told him about Maggie and her rules so the fellas expected some lively banter when he opened the Parade magazine in the canteen at tea time, sure enough, Maggie took it from him as he sat engrossed with it wide open. Startled he said, "What the Fff, ff," and stopped as he spied Maggie holding the mag, "Hang on a minute you cant take that.., its.., my Dad lent it me."

Maggie looked around at the fellas laughing. "He's got you there Maggie ." one of them said. She held a finger up to her eye.., and winked. Pointed at Jesse, "I'll give it to your Mammy when I see her at Mass on Sunday. Get out of that, you lairey little fecker." She smirked.

Finn was making life uncomfortable for Hettie with his persistent familiarity and too close presence. Popping into the canteen often.

Usually into the kitchen area sidling close to Hettie. Maggie as is her wont was quick on the uptake, and mentioned, if she should have a word with him. Hettie shook her head.

"It's a bit awkward, now he's got Connie working with him as his banksman, giving the hand signs to the crane driver.., he told me he would get the crane driver to give Connie some lessons on driving the crane. He uses him as a his gofer... I don't want to mess Connie's chances up, Maggie."

"If he gets to lairey and touchy feely we can soon sort him out, you don't have to put up with his nonsense right.., me darling."

The canteen as run by Hettie and Maggie became a nice friendly welcoming warm and relaxing respite.., from mud and damp conditions of a busy building site. With their bellies full the workers treated the Ladies with almost regal consideration and admiration. So they enjoyed a very contented working life.

A couple of the older and more experience fellas mentioned in passing.., to Maggie, they had cottoned on to what Finns game was, in relation to Hettie.., and if she tipped them the wink, they would sort him out, we can handle it at the moment me darlings, but your very kind, so you are, she said..

A thick old fashioned mist and fog enveloped the Thames, Docklands East End, Stepney, and the whole area was deserted.., only a skeleton staff were on the site. Finn had opened the padlock on the front gates but only opened one side. Connie had followed Finn in and gone off to check the diggings and the crane, as he'd been doing on Finn's orders.

Mr Struthers was the only staffer on site to take charge.

Finn was waiting in the canteen to see if Hettie would be there.

He was in a bad mood, ready to pick a fight.

"I don't know what you two think your doing coming in..,
still now you're here you might as well brew up, the baker
delivered a few rolls.., I've put them in the larder.., you can make
me some Cheese and tomato rolls, do Mr Struthers usual.., he's
turned up and do your Connie something." He stomped out
slamming the door as usual, brisling with aggravation, his
navvy black gang not being in he tried to find a victim, any one
would do, the mood he was in.

He burst into Mr Struthers office making him jump, the
silent foggy atmosphere made everybody nervous.., you never
know if the Rippers

Imitators get fogloopy.

"Oh its you Finn, knock will you.., you frightened the life
out of me."

"Sorry Sir.., so I am.., bad am'nt it?"

"This bloody fog has really given us a problem. I haven't
seen anybody about site. Did you lay every body off.?

"Well the girls turned up, Sir.., so you'll get your nosh and a nice cup of cawfee," He always said cawfee in that way, thought it was funny.

"I thought at least we'd have something to cheer us up so, I didn't have the heart to lay them off, sure we need our brew with this fog, sure its to dark to put your finger in your eye.., so it is."

Finn stomped off and left Mr Struthers to his worries of not keeping to schedule.

The door to the Kitchen burst open, with the same result as when Finn burst in on Mr Struthers, Hettie let out a little shriek.

"Its only meself" He said. They had the radio tuned into to a jokey BBC, who for a laugh were playing a record of Barrell Organ music to give an old time feeling to a Pea Souper Fog Bound Docklands, spookily, just the right atmosphere.., damp, gloomy.., other worldly...

"If you was expecting Burt Lancaster..? How about his double?

Hettie standing at the worktop leaning over, held a roll out, Finn came up behind her reached for the roll pressing him self suggestively against Hettie whilst biting into the roll. Wiggling away she turned facing him.

"Turn it up Finn, that's enough."

Maggie sitting in the enclosed canteen, entered the kitchen from the side door.

"Whats going on.?" She demanded, saw Hettie distressed, and glaring at Finn. Facing him," What the feck you up to.?"

"What you getting stroppy about, I was only being friendly to her."

"Don't get on your high horse with me." He shouted back.

"Remember what I've done for the two of you's."

He stomped out of the canteen angrily stuffing the roll in his donkey jacket pocket slamming the door.

"Lock up after me, and sling you hook for the day." He shouted back.

"Sorry." Hettie said feeling miserable. "He just got to much for me, trying it on all the time, "Sorry. Now I've finally told him, we could be out of work. Sorry Maggie." "That's allright me darling.., yon maggot had to be told. He'll get his comeuppance, one of these days... The way he's going."

With the fog still being thick on the ground, Connie opened up the site.

Finn had told him, after his ruck with the Ladies, to go home after locking up, and unlock, if it was still foggy the next morning.

He pushed open one of the pair of gates and checked the doors to the offices and the canteen were locked. He made his way across a deserted miserable muddy dripping site. Checking the crane door was locked.., and going to look down on the diggings.., he lent on the top of the access ladder, just making out what looked like a bracing timber had fallen with one end leaning into the bottom of the diggings. The fog and mist still thick but swirling his heart missed a beat as in a momentary gap he saw Finn lying on his back, flat out by the end of the bracing timber in the bottom of the diggings. The fog thickened and he strained his eyes hoping it was his imagination. Waiting to see if the fog cleared, his knees all atremble, forced himself to go down and investigate. He climbed down the access ladder…

"Finn.., you alright Finn., Finn." He whispered. Running in his wellington boots as best he could to Finn.., keeping half an eye on the dangerous fallen Bracing timber.., He called again "Finn.., You alright mate,?"

Knowing Finn's peculiar sense of humour, he was hoping Finn would open one eye and shout 'gottcha'.

Connie now totally panic stricken.., giving Finn's shoulder a gentle shake.., looking into Finn's muddied face.., he sobbed, eyes and nose running he cuffed his nose on his sleeve, jumped up and made a beeline for the access ladder, climbing as quick as he could, managing to fall over his own feet, he beetled for the site gates.

With nobody else on site he ran home. Fortunately the Tokes only lived local. Hettie getting ready to go in was dressed when Connie banging on the front door got her rushing to see what the fuss was. Connie in between   catching his breath garbled out "Finns dead."

Hettie opened the door sucking in the fog and mist.

Cuffing his runny nose, Connie mumbled "There's been an accident. Finn's dead at the bottom of the diggings… It wasn't me.., I didn't knock the timber off." "What you on about.?" Hettie asked.

"When I was practicing driving the crane.

"Is anybody else there.?." Connie shook his head.

"Right. Come on lets get back there." Hettie stopped, and shouted over her shoulder into the darkened hall way, "Charlie.., go and knock Maggie up, tell her to come up to the canteen, as quick as she can, and you better come with her.?"

Hettie bustled off swiftly, Connie in her wake.., even with his long legs he had a job keeping up, Jogging behind Hettie he kept up his defence, "It wasn't me.., I'm sure it wasn't me who knocked the timber off, I'd have felt a bump on the cables, I only lifted the bucket up and over the diggings and back again.., when nobody was near."

Hettie was to busy concentrating on getting to the site as quickly as possible to listen to Connie's babbling, and avoid anybody in the fog. As they got to the gates Mr Struthers was sitting outside in his parked car. Connie ran over to tell him, breathlessly explaining what had happened to Finn. Mr Struthers told Connie to open the gates, went to get his wellington boots from the boot of his car. Fully booted he signalled for Hettie to open the canteen and ushered the two of them inside following them in.

They settled on a table by the kitchen.

"Now explain slowly whats happened to Finn?"

"It wasn't my fault, honest.., Sir..," Connie started up again.

Looking from one to the other he could see how worried they both were, he gradually coaxed details out of Connie,,"with his repeated and vehement shake of his head, "The accident's not down to me.., Sir."

"I'll put a brew on shall I?" Hettie asked, seeing Mr Struthers nodding, She disappeared into the kitchen, after explaining Charlie, her husband, and Maggie were on their way to help. Connie was given orders to let them on site, wait for the kitchen deliveries, bring them to the kitchen, and go back and lock the gates, do not let anybody on site, if they want me.., phone. He stood by the gates thankful to be doing something. The kitchen deliveries appeared out of the mist, at the gates, Connie ran to the back of the van opened the doors and because the deleted staff meant only two trays of food. The driver said "That's all mate, that's all there is." Connie lifted them out, kneed the doors closed, carefully carried them into the kitchen, placing them on the nearest table, he ran back out to close the gates. Coming back Mr Struthers was waiting outside for him with Charlie, he was told to lead on, they followed in line carefully over to the accident. The site was a dangerous place at any time and in the fog and mist it was doubly dangerous. They followed Connie in a funeral procession slowly.. Connie went down the access ladder first waiting for Mr Struthers at the bottom of the diggings. Charlie stayed at the top by the ladder. Going over to Finn's body, Mr Struthers investigating all around the fallen timber and the body. "Help me turn him over."

Connie sheepishly help turn the body back and front.

Mr Struthers commented, "The only thing I can see is a bloody wound in the mud on the back of the neck, nothing any where else. He looks like he could have fallen on the bracing timber, or one of the steel brackets.., but i cant find any bloody marks." He looked about the diggings, seeing a tarpaulin, covering the shovels and tools. he told Connie to cover the body with it. The three of them made their way back to the canteen, in silence, his brain worked overtime planning some sort of scheme to get out of any investigation of the accident, by the Police and Council Officials. That could take months, and we're already behind on our time limit schedule.

The table nearest the kitchen had been laid with a selection of rolls, mugs milk and sugar. Hettie and Maggie had been busy, almost like the makings for a wake, they waited until the boys came back to make the tea and coffee. The ladies fussed around them, Hettie cut Charlie's rolls in half because of his teeth being dodgy, Connie was so hungry he almost swallowed the rolls in one. Mr Struthers ate more gentlemanly. Once they were feeling a bit more comfortable and warm inside, Mr Struthers looked at each one. With Charlie sitting inside him and Hettie opposite and Connie on the inside of her.

Maggie hovered about, dish cloth in hand, clearing up the tea things. Like most working class Mothers she rarely sat.

Mr Struthers spoke and they all listened.

"We have a problem here in as much as we wouldn't want to drop Connie into an investigation by the police.

"What.., that's not on," Charlie exclaimed.

"It wasn't my fault.., no, no way, it wasn't Dad."

Hettie gasped putting her hand nervously to her mouth, shaking her head.

"look.., lets get this straight.., I don't want to report the death to the Police. Nothing can be done for Finn." Maggie crossed herself. They all glanced up at her with blank expressions. "Anyone got any suggestions.?"

"Why cant he just have tripped over and fell down the hole, or fell off the ladder..,?" Offered Charlie,

"There would still be an investigation. With Finn lying where he is under the fallen timber at the bottom of the diggings.., it would involve your Son.., as it was known he was learning to drive the Crane. The police would ask about the site. No doubt about that."

Mr Struthers looked emphatically from one to the other.

Maggie lurking at the end of the table piped up.

"Go and dump your one in the Thames Sir.., a lot of rubbish ends up in there." They all looked at Maggie shocked. Giggling.

"Maggie.., really..," Exclaimed Hettie tutting.

"It's a thought." Said Mr Struthers smiling shaking his head.

Maggie walking up and down inbetween the tables, flicking her tea towel at none existent flies over the tables.

"Well why not..,? Sir" She glared.

Charlie said "Its worth discussing though isn't it?. With all this fog about we wouldn't be seen, would we? Mind you.., how could we get a big lump like him out?"

"We would need the crane to shift him." looking at Connie, "We cant get the Crane driver. Is it possible you could lift him?" Mr Struthers asked.

"Well I could have a try, I know all the controls." He said enthusiastically. Feeling a bit better.

They all started to feel, with their bellies full, their brains and bodies perking up, suggestions came thick and fast.

Charlie offered his services as a rigger because of similar work he sometimes does at the docks, he had seen slings and strops with the tools in the diggings near where Finn lay.

Mr Struthers thought things might not.., be.., to bad. His management skills started working.

"You were in Finns black gang for the last couple of months.., and I know Finn was happy with you.. I reckon you and your Dad could get Finn out." He said looking from Connie and nodding at Charlie. Who shaking his head said.

"No Sir., you've got to be with us all the way, or nothing doing."

"Take him to Shadwell Park, be easier to drop him in behind the Rotherhithe tunnel stairs roundhouse. I know how to take the chain and pad lock off the gate to the park, they keep it closed in the fog." Was Connie's suggestion. "We could get him there in your car, Sir.."

"No No, we mustn't leave any individual traces."

"Well how will we get him there?." Charlie queried. "Use one of the site wheel barrows." Connie said.

"They've all been stamped with the site name, when Finn goes in the Thames we don't want to bring anything back that could be connected back here."

They had a group thinking session, the little grey cells were jumping in and out of the collective brain boxes hoping to settle on a eureka moment. Carrying him was out of the question, to big and heavy. Maggie volunteered her big old pram. They chuckled at that. She was hurt at them laughing at her. Until she explained the life her pram had led.., and the stuff she'd shifted in it.., apart from her eight kids.

"That old pram has held sacks of coal, would you believe.., sacks of tatties.., big tins of all sorts.., that my old man or my boys found lying about in the Docks. The Gate keepers and Coppers thought I was a lovely old Gel meeting the old man.., when the security was distracted they loaded the pram up with the babbies in it. The Gatemen didn't look in a pram for fear of being shyicked by the Dockers. They don't make proper prams these days.., so they don't, not at all.., You can chuck it.., anyway.., my girls wouldn't be seen dead wheeling a relic, like my old pram, as they call it.

Mr Struthers with his co conspirators set out the plans. Himself and Charlie would go down the diggings and rig Finn up with a sling under the arms and around the back of his body so that at least he would look dignified coming out of the diggings head up.

They all had torches.., a necessity in foggy days. Hettie would stand at the top of the diggings by the access ladder, she could then look down and see Mr Struthers torch signal, one long flash, then look back to signal Connie in the crane, with two flashes, start the crane then lift.

Rigging a big man like Finn was no easy matter, turning his body back and front in the dark, foggy and damp sodden earth. With a final heave he was ready. Hettie nervous and tense, looking down at a scene that could have been from her childhood war horrors, blinking with tears in her eyes from the thoughts.., and fog.., saw one long flash of the torch.., she turned towards the crane and flashed twice.

The noise from the crane shattered the atmosphere, almost feeling that it would clear the fog. Just like a monster fishing, they watched mesmerised as the fishing line went taught and Finn appeared head first out of the diggings slowly, arms slightly out from his side, Maggie standing behind Connie in the crane with her hands on his shoulders coaxing him along, "Good boy yourself.., steady sonny.., steady, good boy.., concentrate.., your doing a grand job.., so you are."

Seeing the body in the misty fog swinging slightly, looking enormously magnified and ghostly.

Connie with tears in his eyes, steeling himself to concentrate, listened to Maggie as she whispered a prayer. "Holy Mary Mother of God"

As she blessed herself. They both said 'God bless' together.

"Jesus Mary and Joseph.., would you ever look at that..," Blessing herself again. Connie swung the body out and around as Mr Struthers and Charlie clambered up the access ladder and moved over in front of the crane as Connie lowered the body down. Charlie quickly undid the slings around Finn and threw them under the crane. Signalling for Connie to cut the crane motor off. A deathly silence fell over the site as befitting a bereavement. Hettie mouthed to Mr Struthers as she passed him, "I'm going back to the canteen."

"What A Phantasmagorical Spectre..," Connie exclaimed.

"What the fekkin hell you on about boy?" Maggie said.

"My girl friend Lena, says that, thought Wapping was full of that sort of thing because of old movies." Connie switched every thing off in the crane. Full of himself he jumped out of the crane intending to hand Maggie safely down unfortunately he tripped landing in a heap onto the muddy ground with a splat.

"Mind what you're doing you big eedjit.., you nearly had me over."

Connie looked up at Maggie standing in the doorway of the crane.

"Sorry Mrs O'Connell." He brushed himself down, gingerly stood up, handing Maggie down as gentlemanly as he could.

She helped brush him down tut tutting Motherly.

"Well done me darling, you did well son."

Looking at Connie reminded of her youngest son Albert, killed in the war at nineteen, on the Atlantic convoys. Smiling she said," Come on melkshem, we'd better get moving, your Mums gone to the canteen."

Connie ran over to help Charlie and Mr Struthers ease Finn into a site wheelbarrow, his legs hung over all ways, but they could move him.

Gathering in the canteen the next part of the procedure had to be organized. Mr Struthers thought so far so good. Charlie had mentioned the top of the tide on the Thames would be about twelve o'clock. It would be better.., for all concerned.., if Finn was taken by the tide.., back around Millwall and down Barking way.., and possibly a trip to Canvey Island.., that will be a nice holiday for him, Charlie sniggered...

Maggie offered to get her pram as time was getting on. Mr Struthers agreed that would help. "Would you like me to accompany you in the fog? Mrs O'Connell" He offered. "Bless you sir.., I've walked these streets of Shadwell and Wapping since me Mammy and Da brought us over from Cork, me only being nine, I think.., so I wont be frightened of a wee bit of fog. No I'll be fine.., sure.., it'll be a brave man who'll jump on me…"

After Maggie returned with Finn's Funeral hearse ., pram. Mr Struthers set out the plan.

What I suggest is once we put Finn into the pram we get a move on. Hettie and Maggie stay here, they can lock the main gates after we're gone, if they wouldn't mind," They both nodded. "Then ladies.., back and have a well deserved cuppa in the canteen.., until we return."

"Charlie can push the pram, myself an Connie take a bit of the weight off the pram by supporting it each side."

"Be a bit suspicious.., a bunch of geezers mooching about in the fog wont it.?" Charlie thoughtfully mentioned.

"I tell you what.., what about if we make out we're bevvied up, and talk with an Irish accent?" Connie enthused.

"Good idea Son.., I've heard you doing a good take off, of old Finn."

Mr Struthers said, "Terrific idea Lads, but my Irish accent is pretty bad.., I suppose I could mumble feckin eejits.., every now and again leaving you two to do all the drunken chatter. Most people will steer clear of a bunch of Irish when they're sossled.., and no mistake ."

Connie found an old cap in the canteen. In his Donkey Jacket and boots, he suggested they left any talking to him, that's if anybody looked like getting close to them.., and why not call him Finn.., in that case…

Now the plans were set Mr Struthers detailed the route they would take.

"From Stepney Way.., Go down Jubilee Street. You live there.., I believe, so you'd better walk in the middle of the road, just in case you bump into anyone on the pavement and they recognize your good selves. Head down to Commercial Road there might be a few cars as you cross the road so you might have to use your torches a bit more, into to Sutton Street.., we'll hopefully be getting more used to lugging Finn along so we can get a shift on.., torches on again as we cross Cable Street.., just in case of traffic, nip down King David Lane.., cross The Highway to the other side of the road left along The Highway and we should be at Shadwell Park Gates. With a bit of luck and the fog still thick and dense, we will have got the most difficult part of our exercise and possible exposure almost finished."

"Mr Struthers Sir.., we do know how to get to Shadwell Park., blimey we've been going there for donkeys years..," Charlie sounding a bit miffed.

"I know Charlie .., but I've been describing the route for my sake as well, I don't come from here., sorry if I offended you."

By the time they had got to the Park gates they were exhausted. The journey had, for Charlie and Mr Struthers been a nervous trial, not for Connie who was as high as a kite, he unhooked the gate chain and broken padlock.., and in they trundled. By now the pram wheels were squeaking pitifully.., despite Maggie saying she rubbed plenty of dripping around the axle's. With the noise from the pram, and three ghostly figures effin and blindin in Irish accents.., its no surprise.., everybody stayed well clear.

Shadwell Park was ghostly quiet.., the mist and fog from The Thames and the top of the turning tide, made a disquieting uneasy atmosphere.

They wheeled the pram around the Rotherhithe Tunnel Round House to The Thames guard rail. Looking down into the water they had a quiet reflection. They were hidden behind the Round house from the Park, not that anybody would be

mad enough to be there, in thick fog, apart from these three meschugeners. Connie as a child played running games around the Roundhouse, so couldn't resist thoughtlessly trotting around it a few times…, while the Boss and his Dad rested. Charlie looked at Mr Struthers, then at Finn in the pram.

"We ready?.." Mr Struthers nodded sombrely.., the seriousness of what they were doing getting more intense.

Charlie whispered "Connie.., where are you.., you silly little git.., for gawd sake." He sprinted back to the pram "Sorry." He muttered cheerfully.

They gathered around Finn. Mr Struthers and Connie lifted the arms and body, Charlie lifted the legs.., heaved him up onto the guardrail and over went Finn into a watery End.., with a surprisingly gentle splash.

Mr Struthers said "Good bye Finbarr Coen.., I'll remember you.., you did well by me ." "God bless Finn." Connie whispered. "You got nothing to say Dad.?". "You got what you deserved you Fenian barsterd."

"Dad..," Connie exclaimed. "Anybody who plants bombs on us is a shitbag." Charlie spat. Connie picked the pram up and threw it into The Thames to join the other hundreds of assorted pieces of junk.

Charlie and Mr Struthers lent over the guardrail to watch as the outgoing tide took a slowly sinking body passed Free Trade Wharf, and they hoped out of London Dockland. Connie was waiting by the gates, he'd had enough, waiting impatiently juggling the chain and padlock. As soon as they walked out through the gates, he shut and chained them. They hurried back to the Stepney Way site, very mournfully, no words spoken.

Charlie tossed a pebble against the side of the canteen as a call for the main gates to be opened. Hettie ran eagerly out to let the boys in. She looked into each of their eyes.., nervously.., queryingly.

"Everything go alright..?" She whispered." "Cause it did." Charlie barked. The Ladies had prepared the teas and rolls again.., fussing around the three musketeers affectionately.., especially Connie.

They all eat ravenously the nervous tension gradually lessening sup and bite by sup and bite.

Mr Struthers started the inquest on the best way forward.

As the site Engineer and Finn's Boss it was his duty to collate any evidence the Police might want, if and when his body washed up.., "Sorry ladies for being a bit indelicate." Maggie told the story of the full ash trays in the morning in the canteen.., someone was using the canteen at night. Charlie mentioned that his brother, Izzy, got wind of Finn running card games in here. Some very nasty bits of work used to meet Finn in one of the Maltese gangs Boozers., down Wapping High Street, In fact we came across the same three in The Earl of Essex, Manor Park one night, Irish they was, very likely IRA.

Mr Struthers shook his head. "I'm shocked, I had no idea, what he was up to. I wonder if they had anything to do with Finn's accident? It's a thought, isn't it.?" Maggie dropped another bomb shell by telling about some of the dog ends in the ash trays had lipstick on them.

"That's right is it not?" She looked at Hettie, who nodded shyly. Maggie said "We don't wear lipstick as you can see.., Sir.., but I've got a good idea who it might be.., two of the Maltese tarts from up that way is the gruesome twosome, Bumbussel Flo and Tarty Tina, and as you know Finn's always at it with any old scrubber. We didn't find any empty beer bottles, he made sure to clear those away."

"Could you turn off the radio?," Mr Struthers asked Hettie. They hadn't noticed until he said the barrel organ music being played again was getting just to creepy.., after all our diversions. Hettie apologized with a laugh the others joined her, relieving the tension giggling.

Maggie looked at Hettie, and said "Will you tell him ?" Hettie declined with a shake of her head.

"Is there something else I should know,?"

"Well.., Sir.., Finn has been trying it on with herself.., Hettie, so he has, even threatening.., not a nice man the gobshite, begging your pardon.., Sir..,

"The more I'm finding out the more I've given to much power to Mr Coen.., by the looks of things.

Connie joined in the general slander, "I don't know if you know, Sir.., but he expected his black gang to give him a bung every pay night."

"I had an idea that happened, it's a practice I meant to put a stop to, but never got round to.., but I will now."

Now that Finn Coen's shenanigans were out Connie said Winston had been seen in a pub with Flo and the other one, probably the same pub where Finn met for fixing the card games up. Although him and Winston did have a ruck on site. I don't think there was any loved lost between them, but Winston might Know something, you never know.

"He did ask me if he could do a bookie runners job on site, so as he was being honest and if it didn't interfere with his work, that's fine." Mr Struthers explained. "But I will expect him to tell me anything he knows. I'm sorry about Finns nonsense Mrs Toke if I had have known I would have delt with him." He said smiling apologetically.

A quiet nervous hush came over the canteen as everybody relaxed, Mr Struthers breathed a sigh of relief.

"I think we could all do with own homes I think. I will give every one a days pay today, you as well Mr Toke.

I hope to see you Ladies, and Connie tomorrow. If you lock up Connie. Good night every one and thank you so much." He trudged out tiredly, fagged out, exhausted.

At home after a day like no other. Hettie sank into the old armchair thankfully, her sigh of relief put a sympathetic smile on Connie and Charlie's face, who said, "That's right Gel.., you have a good old kip, I reckon we done well.., don't you.?"

Hettie, eyes closed, drifting off.., smiled dreamily, waived a hand airily.

"I'm going out to meet Lena.., if that's okey." Connie said.

"Do you good to get out." Hettie mumbled.., eyes closed.

"I'll have a wander, as well.., I think.., see if I can find our Izzy.., bound to be in one of the music pubs.., itching to do a turn."

Hettie opened one eye, looking from one to the other.

"Remember you two.., wartime words.., Be like Dad keep Mum.., make sure.., shtum."

"I know nuffink..," Charlie laughed. The pair walked out, leaving Hettie gratefully alone.

Hettie completely immersed in a memory of her mother singing one of their favourite lullaby songs, (Vilja, O Vilja, The Witch Of The Woods,

Would I Not Die For You Dear If I Could,

Vilja, O Vilja, My Love And My Bride,

Softly And Sadly He Sighed,)

In the warm loving family East End home, her Mothers voice came gently.., carrying Hettie off.., humming along.., In their usual wonderful encompassing daydream, Hettie immersed childishly with Mutti.

Their loving Aura wrapped around them..,(Sube.., Liebling.., God Bless.., are you well?) 'Yes thank you Mutti. We have had a bit of a day, yesterday and.., today. I have some confessions I would like you to hear.' (As Poppa and I always taught you sweetie, confession is a cleansing of the soul, and if its like your last perplexing stories.., I can put your mind at ease..,)

'The man who got myself and Connie the jobs here has made some threats, if I'm not nice to him.., I lost my temper, and shouted at him.., we had words.'

(Its unlike you to row. Even as a Child sweetie you were always demure.)

'He's not a very nice man, Momma, some times calls my Brethren.., Brits, sneeringly. The other day we had a ruck in the Canteen.., he locked the gates, after showing Maggie off site, she finishes before me. He came back into the Kitchen and made close contact with me, threateningly.., saying in a snide way that if we couldn't work as a team he might have to get someone who would. I'm a good friend to have, he said.., with a smirk.., I could be a big help.., in more ways than one.., if you know what I mean. Wouldn't you know. He winked, obviously Charlie cant give a lively Lady all she needs.., not much jizz there, so there's not.

He pushed up close and made a grab for me.., you know where Mutti.., I pulled away in surprise., and gasped, covering up. He put a big filthy grin on his face.., well.., well.., well...i knew there was something about yourself.., would you believe it sure am'nt this a turn up for the books. He stared at me with a sickening grin, secrets is it.., now.., now.

A noise from the site stopped his nonsense. That must be your Son he sniggered. I'll send Connie home.., you wait here till I come back. I'm sure you'll be more friendly to old Finn.., when I get back.., and went out slamming the door.

I was in a quandary Momma.., what shall I do...?

Connie came into the kitchen minutes later, saying.., He just told me to go home and lock the gates after me. So if your finished I can walk you home for a change.

Where's he gone ?, was all I could think.., to ask Connie.., He shrugged his shoulders, and said. Finn went over by the crane then said he was going to check no one was down the diggings.

Momma I was so angry with this Finn Coen. I told Connie to go out of the kitchen and wait for me into the canteen. There's a shopping bag of goodies I left on a table.., that I was taking home. Some rolls in there if your hungry, I told Connie.

Momma my temper was at boiling point.., I picked up a carving knife.., and juggled it about..., then I picked up a wooden rolling pin, I waved it about.., then made up my mind.

I'm going a toilet.., I shouted to Connie.., wait there till I get back.

Still holding the rolling pin I ran out after Finn.., the fog was still pretty thick so I had to look for the misty image of the crane and carefully watch where I trod.., until I could see an obscure shape of somebody standing by the ladder *to the diggings, looking down. As I got near, I kicked some rubble down into the diggings.., Finn leant over the top of the ladder at the noise of the rubble cascading down. He didn't hear me come up behind him, I hammered the rolling pin with all my strength at the back of his stretched out neck.., he grunted, and as he fell.., I gave him a push..., his body fell crashing against one of the big wooden beams..., dislodging one end, his body somersaulted, landing flat on his back. I thought the beam was going to land on Finn, but the dislodged end landed beside him.*

Momma my heart was beating so fast.., I looked down at Finn's body flat on his back, not moving.., with his arms and legs slightly outstretched.., in the hazy bottom of the atmospheric foggy diggings, he looked like a huge giant.

I had to drag myself away from the dramatic scene.., and stumble, shakily back to the canteen. The phosphorescent sooty smell and taste in the air, and the deed.., almost made me sick.

Lets go.., I bustled in at Connie. Take the bag.., open the gates while I lock up the canteen.

With that, we lost no time in getting off site.

Walking home, the pair of us were very very subdued.'

(Sweetie this story is very dramatic . I remember those tales of yours when you were little and the way you were so convinced every word was true. Honest Mutti, you used to say honest, honest, until I said Harti I believe you. Don't scold me Sube.., when I remember your little face I see my Harti.., my daring little Harti.

But.., Hettie. You are.., sweetie.., Only Momma knows.)

'Mutti you are naughty, but I forgive you, as I should, can I be forgiven such deadly deeds.?'

(Of course, of course, of course, Our beautiful dreams will always stay as they should.., in our hearts.)

***

Father Pat's after Mass tea party was its usual gossipy noise laden affair, until Father came along the length of the table, a big smile on his face. Everyone waiting for the personal greeting and warm cheering word to make their Sunday morning a satisfying reason to be at Mass and feeling quite Holy. A heartfelt handshake and tender smile to every neighbour within touching distance in the Pews, and a 'Peace be with you' at the end of the Mass.., was a nice way for an introduction to Father's Hooley.., as he would say.

Is it yourself? He said to one. Now what have you been up too.., you rascal? He would say to another. The Allotment going well? Alfonzo.., he joked. To old Alfie Herring.., who's corpulent stomach shook the table laughing. Glory be is it not the terrible twins.., Maggie and her sidekick Hettie.., would you Adam and Eve it.., Begorroh.

"You're a terrible man, so you are." Maggie answered back laughing.

As Father worked his way around the table.

Maggie turned to Hettie," I don't know if your interested in a bit of waitressing work darling, I've been offered a job at a dinner dance for a council do, at the town hall. Cash in hand, good little number, so."

Sitting side by side the Ladies had to converse, leaning close to each other, because of the noise from the rest of the enthralled parishioners sitting enjoying the fair of the Fathers teas, and his banter.

"I haven't ever waited on table before." Answered Hettie.

"Its no problem, I'll be plating up so you can help me by getting the food ready. Then only if they get too busy would you wait on table. And of course, clearing up once the gannets have finished." Smiling with a nod of the head. "Your Charlie is going to be there.., head gofer and washer upper."

"Is he?"

"Sorry love, didn't he tell you? I saw him up Cable Street .., the other day. Men.., don't know whether their on their arse or their elbow.., away with the fairies most of the time.

I tell you what.., why not ask Connie and Lena. Make it a Toke, Beano."

That set the ladies giggling and laughing.

With Father Pat busy chatting away, Hettie glanced at him.., put her hand over her mouth and turning to Maggie whispered..,

"While their all busy nattering I'm shooting off, Connie's bringing Lena home for dinner, so I want to get home and get the dinner on."

"I'll get meself gone as well I'm thinking. My Mary and Norah are coming round.., they'll help my Carol get things going so they will, sure it'll all be done by the time I get home.., aye and pigs might fly."

The Ladies rose together. Walking out arm in arm they called their goodbyes. Getting back the Tat ta's, toodle oo's, cheerio's, and see ya.

Maggie O'Connell the Toke's all spranced up in white shirts and black trousers or skirts, as the case might be, on duty in the waiting room. Next door to the Assembly room.

In Poplar Town Hall, Poplar High Street. Dockside East London.

Charlie busy lugging in the food containers. The Ladies and the one Waiter, namely Connie, along for the giggle he reckoned.., little does he know… The Assembly room tarted up a bit for the grateful thank you, 'Do'.., to a long serving slum clearance Engineer.., or in Council parlance Urban Planning expert.., one Lester Seed 'mustard or muzzy' to his few friends. A studied deliberate verisimilitude pose, with mad professor bald head, excitable eyebrows, melancholy grey eyes, ready full toothed grin, five nine in height, stooped important affected bearing. Proud to shop at Burtons The Discernible Tailors For Men.

Plus the defining spotted bow tie.

Joining the council at Twenty Five years of age, he was a veteran of Thirty years of internal pen pushers squabbling.., in his opinion he deserved the honour of a dinner/dance with Ikey Figgis Four, Band.., with Izzy Toke.., Guest Artiste...

Able to choose who sits with him at the top table he very naturally chose his ally and confidante..., Julian Cuttle.., all five six in height, and hefty.., pushy spiteful aggravation. Suited and booted in shiny Blue Mohair Italian suit, Pastel Grey waisted Shirt, Gold Cufflinks, Italian handmade shoes, silk tie elegantly folded pocket silk handkerchief. Perry Como styled dyed fair hair permed. Haulage and Building Contractor. Swaggering and swanky lairy cockney accent. Himself and his overblown gawd blimey Missus.., Effie.., both late forty's in age.., not admitted by either.

Herself.., same height as her old man, a little on the large size, dressed in matching mini skirted grey Mohair suit, short dark hair.., Dusty Springfield style.., gold hooped earrings.., gold chained crucifix, shell cameo brooch, gold charm bracelet, full of gold charms from foreign travels. They all arrived in Julian Cuttle's Racing green Mark two, Jaguar two point four auto.

Making their way to the top table beside the band, they made the most of what they hoped was a grand entrance with the royal wave and acknowledging smile. Unfortunately nobody played a blind bit of notice of them. The band was playing and the guests were gossiping and no doubt slandering each other departments, as is the usual case.

Joining Mr Lester Seed on the top table as his last special guest, Bertie Roseman a long term employee in the same department, very similar in appearance, could almost be a younger brother but with sandy coloured hair. Beholding to Lester Seed for covering up a sticky planning application deal he got caught in. Thanks to Mr Seed's influence..., it got put in the back burner and forgotten.

All seated at the top table smiling benignly, friendly small talk, while patiently waiting what for them will be a free treat..

But for the rest a couple of quid for a pair of tickets, half price kids. Roast.., beef or chicken veg.., and sweet. Glass of sauterne wine or soft drink hopefully big nosh up, why else would they be there. Bring your own drinks after meal though. The noise in the hall just simmering gently.

Julian and Effie giving the biggen, waiving greeting to different tables.

"Blimey Julian you know more people at my Hooley than I do". Lester laughed.

"I bought a dozen tickets for my drivers and their families. Couldn't let your big night go without a bit of a swing, could I? Muzzy me old son..,"

"Actually I didn't want a turn out like this, when the Chief floated the idea of doing something for me in thanks.., for my long service. I said a couple of tickets for the Opera at Covent Garden would do nicely.., in fact, I heard my favourite Opera Rigoletto might be coming on ..,"

Julian butted in, "Riggy 'bleed'n who.?" Lester burst out laughing.

Effie snapped "Riggle eto ..., you ignoramus..,"

Lester, shoulders shaking with laughter, said." Mind you I'd have had to get someone to go with me if they did get me tickets."

"Don't look at me son..," Julian shook his head. "I've got enough with the old boiler in doors shrieking her guts off."

Effie punched him on the arm. "You saucy bleeder."

"Not you.., my love .., I mean your bleed'n Muvver."

"Oh.., right.., that's alright then". Effie leant over the table and patted Lester's hand. "I'd always go with you Les, I could do with a bit of culture down me lugholes."

Bertie Roseman enjoying the banter.., laughing, "I did try Lester, but they said the tickets for the Opera would cost too much. All though I was given the task to organise things, they even queried the entertainment.., such as it is..,

The Ikey Figgis Four were playing softly a selection of pop songs when Bertie Roseman waved a hand in their direction. Ikey looked over at him and nodded. They started playing a specially arranged set.

Bertie explained. "Ikey is playing his 'Dinner Music,' its eight o'clock and there about to serve dinner so he's arranged.., as he said in, 'Andante cantabile'.., time, 'Variations on a theme of Harry Champion'

Do you think I should announce it?" The diners hungrily expecting their dinner were whispering and looking happily for the waiters.

Julian butted in as usual, "What the bleedin hell is he on about? Ikey Figgis was always two bob short of a pound."

The band tinkled away merrily with Professor Ikey Figgis on keyboard and his band playing.., Boiled Beef and Carrots.., I want Meat.., Hot Meat Pie, Saveloy, and Trotters, Home made Sausages, I've got a lovely Bunch Of Coconuts, and a few more of 'our Arry's' gems.

"Right.., lets be having you.., time to earn your shekels." Doreen Levy the Manageress of the Caterers said importantly.

"Maggie get your team organized and ready.., me and my sister Lettie will waite on the top table. We've a special surprise starters, a tray of small dishes.., the main man is a bit of a gourmet so I've made half a dozen different types of appetizers for him and his guests. We've got

A small dish of Gefilte Fish Balls, a small dish of Caviar, a small dish of smoked Salmon, a small dish of Jellied Eels, a small dish of Prawn Cocktails, and the last one.., Curried Cockles in Sushi..,

That should get them going, if that don't nothing will.., right gel's"

Lettie, Maggie, Hettie and Lena.., The Ladies giggling with relief as the nervous tension eased.

Doreen handed the tray of gastronomic delights to Charlie to mind.

"Hold on to them Chas.., we don't want them to disappear after all the work I put in. Thanks sweetie." And gave him a winning smile.

Charlie couldn't be more pleased.., 'everything falling nicely into place' he chuckled evilly. 'So Muzzy Seed is a bit of a gourmet connoi.., sewer, I'll give him connoi., bleedin., sewer of nosh. See how he gets on with my mouse repellent from the allotment. A touch of Foxglove, Wolfbane, Belladonna, Monkshood, and a smidgin of what he thinks he is one of, Lord and Ladies. All ground up together in a powder with a drop of my own brew of Poteen to make a nice dry paste.., just the right ingredients to be kept in an empty small glass meat paste pot. Should give him the two bob bits for a day or two. Cackling to himself,

Connie interrupted his concentration, "You all right there Dad?"

"Yes I'm fine, just taking care of these delicate dishes, must be perfect for the nobs, mustn't they..?"

"how you getting on Son.?" Connie smiled back. "Okey Dad."

Charlie looked around, placed the special tray on a worktop, with his back to the rest.., saw every body was too busy to notice what he was doing and spooned a dollop of his revenge mixture onto all the delicacies quite artistically that they looked part of the design. A memory of years ago before the war, of a black and white Film, the witches in Macbeth cackling Hubble bubble.., he chuckled.., blimey.., just like me.

"Right me darling's.., I'm off to do the top table. Lettie you do the table opposite, Maggie get your team taking orders following us, get Charlie to help plating up. Charlie when I come back.., I'll take the tray of goodies out. Is it all right?"

Charlie nodded emphatically. "That's my boy." She winked at him.

Seeing movement from the waiters the diners gee'd them selves up expectantly, a happy buzz went around the few Ladies who were dancing with their kids, the little ones happily, the older boy's grumpily ran back to their tables, sitting expectantly, eating irons at the ready getting advice from their mothers what to order, sit up straight and stop fidgeting.

Hettie, Lena, And Connie had the job of going around each table giving a drink to each diner. They had the choice of Sauterne, Orangeade or Lemonade. Doreen went to the top table for their order.

"Hello Ladies and Gentlemen hope your all well." With her best smile, some would say gushing. They nodded and smiled in unison.

"We have a little surprise for you Mr Seed.., Mr Roseman told me you're a Gourmet," She smiled around at the others, and a nod and raised eyebrows? at Mr Roseman, who nodded yes, smiling at Mr Seed. She took their order. "Shan't be a moment." And swiftly walked off to the plating room. "Charlie.., lets be having you, 'tout suite' where's goodies? You been looking after them?"

Charlie came bustling up, handing the gourmet tray over with a silly curtsy and a twisty grin. "Course.., with my life.., already.."

"Museltov.., You saucy monkey." Doreen said, laughing.

She took the covered tray and a bottle of Sauterne back to the top table. And flamboyantly presented the Gourmet delicacies with a plate of bread rolls. Dramatically removing the cover. The table were not sure at what was presented, one might say underwhelmed, but they smiled indulgently.

True to form Julian said "What's this lot.., smells a bit Fishy to me."

"That looks very nice my dear." Effie said to Doreen., glaring at Julian.., smiling at Lester, then Bertie

All systems go as the waiting staff bustled about serving the dinners. Whispered chatter broken by the odd child announcing 'I don't like that', and Mother snapping 'leave the bleeding thing,' then looking around embarrassed at the show of temper. Other table's glancing at her sympathetically.

Mr Seed sampling the Caviar first, looked around his table smiling.

"This is quite good. Come on everybody.., Try and have a taste of the different samples.., you might enjoy some."

Julian pipped up, "If your game.., Muzzy.., I might as well be poisoned with you..," As he broke a bread roll in half, dipping from one dish tasting it, then on to another.

Bertie said apologetically, "I think I'll wait for my Chicken dinner, thanks.., bit of a dicky tummy."

The Band competing with the noise from happy eaters.., gallantly tried to give Ikey Figgis's 'Dinner Music' a decent hearing but in a competition between 'Darby Kelly and 'lugholes.., blowing out your Kite wins.., every time.

Julian getting a fondness for the Gourmet dishes tried every one. Any excuse to have a gulp of wine. Effie had a two Gefilte fish balls.., and Jellied Eels, tried Smoked Salmon but took the spoonful back out of her mouth and put it on Julian side plate with a shudder, "No.., Cant eat that." She mumbled. Julian smirked at her. "Piggy Ragin."

"Nuts". came the reply.

Surprisingly most of the dishes were eaten. The Cockles in Sushi, invented by Doreen, got left, along with the Smoked Salmon and most of the Prawn Cocktails.

Charlie keeping a wary eye on the top table saw them sit back in their chairs, finished with their starters.

"Connie.., Connie…, go and pick that tray of Goodies from the top table." Charlie whispered. "Whats that Dad?" Connie asked.

"Go out and ask them if they are finished, politely. Then bring all the cutlery and dishes back to me". Connie looked at his Father quizzically.

Charlie whispered forcefully, "Don't look at me in that old fashioned way, do what your told."

"Alright.., Alright.., I'm going"

"Well.., Lester, I think you deserve this celebration of all the good work you've done for the Dockers.., getting a lot them out of the slums they inhabited." Bertie said ingratiatingly. He looked at Effie and Julian for approval smiling.

They both nodded. "Well said.., Bertie..," They acknowledged.

"You've been a right diamond geezer. If you don't mind me saying so..," Julian said.

Effie leant over the table squeezing Lester's hand. "You've been a God send to the Cockneys of East London.., right enough. Even though some of the toerags don't appreciate what you've done for the area."

"I have had some abusive comments and letters, but I took no notice as I was sure I was doing right." Lester acknowledge.

"When I signed off a street for slum clearance.., I knew I was going to get them a lovely flat with all the mod-coms for comfortable easy living. Who would want to live in an old falling down dump with outside toilet, no bathroom. Some of the old houses didn't even have electric installed. Some complained they grew up in their old house I'm not sure that's something to boast about, getting rheumatism.., or pneumonia from your home. Much better to live in a nice clean environment in a well designed High Rise Block."

Connie waiting patiently for Lester to finish lecturing the table. Asked.

"Shall I clear the tray of starters away,?"

Lester with a wave of his hand and an affirmative nod., yes.

"Mind you.., the Ronen Point High Rise Flats, in Canning Town collapsing.., was a disaster." Bertie pointed out.

"Should never allowed the tenants to put gas cookers or any gas appliance in the flats. Should never have given them the choice. All Electric only. Planners were idiots.., cant let tenants dictate. The tenants could have been installing Gas appliances themselves. I've been in slum clearance for thirty five.., years I've always been against Gas in High Rise." Lester agitated and red faced.., sheepishly apologised. "Sorry about that.., one of my hobby horses. Absolutely no gas in any Tower block."

Connie back in the plating room gave Charlie the tray of starter left overs and cutlery. Charlie grabbed the tray, emptied the slops into a grease proof bag, then into his old holdall. He was just dropping the cutlery and dishes into a container for dirty dishes, to go back for automatic dish washing to the caterers. When a deep voice behind, made him jump.

"Hello.., Hello.., Charlie whats to do?" Charlie looked around startled.

"Gawd help us.., its your self Mr Rivett, you startled me.., how you doing? See you managed to get a ticket for this shindig.., Sergeant."

Sergeant Ron 'Rusty' Rivett.., local well known copper, font of all knowledge in the Docklands of any shifty nonsense.

"Whatsit.., give me a ticket.., you know whatsname? The little one of the poison dwarf twins." Charlie laughed.

"How do you remember the Villain's, with a brain like a sieve?"

"Charlie.., Its all up there in my big head." Sergeant Rivett said tapping the side of his head and winking.

"It's a fair old do, so it is. Dinner alright. I meant to come and see you before. You remember that Mick.., Finn, whatsit? The investigation's over into the drowning.., officially.., an accident because he was Kaylied, plastered. Unofficially.., the word is.., the I.R.A, done him. We had some weird tales about a body being wheeled down to the Thames in a pram.., I wish locals would lay off the sauce. Whats the chance of a body as big as Chummy in a pram.., being wheeled about East London and not being seen by us Coppers? Chas.., a favour to ask? Can you wrap up some of leftover Meat or Chicken for the Old Ladies pets."

Charlie shook hands with Sergeant Rivett." Course I can Sarge, my pleasure."

Doreen came bustling in. Passing the sergeant on his way out.

"What did he want..? Rusty..,"

"Just some scraps for his old women's pets." Said Charlie. "You know what the 'old bill' are like.., always on the scrounge."

"Right Boys and Gels. Everything is swinging, we're going great guns. Connie you carry on with Lena and see to the top table.., Hettie will you help my Sister and do whats left. I reckon we've got this sorted. I'll go round and see if there's any moans.., I dare erm."

The waiters had started bringing the dirty diches back to the plating area. Charlie was going to be busy putting the leftover food into a pigswill container, and the dishes and cutlery into the dirty dishes, container. Maggie was like a banshee clearing the dirty dishes and cutlery. Humming and singing along to the faint sound from the Ikey Figgis Band coming from the Main room.

Connie was getting a lot of attention from Effie at the top Table," Your looking very tasty dressed up. Has anybody told you, you look a bit like Michael Caine.., Your Charlie Tokes son aren't you?"

Julian listening to his wife while eyeing up Lena, and winking at her.

"He must get his looks from his Mother." He laughed looking at Connie. "Take no notice of him love, he's pig ignorant." Said Effie patting Connie's arm.

Connie smiling at the banter. Looked at Lena raising his eyebrows.

"You could be right there," He said.

Julian asked if Lena and Connie were together, Lena smiled and nodded. I thought you were, you make a good team. If you ever want a job.., come and see me, I can always use good workers. He gave off what he thought was his 'billy big time' impression.

Mr Seed waved his hand over the table for Connie to clear away the dishes. Connie did what was indicated and started clearing away the finished meals. Mr Seed told him he didn't want any sweet, the others agreed. Effie had started taking bottles of drink out of her expensive leather bag she had carried in, placing them on the table in front of Julian.., indignantly. Effie had brought half a dozen of her best cut glass tumblers. Julian placed a glass in front of each person and began pouring a ball of Jameson's for Lester, who winked at Julian.., 'you know my tipple well'.., he smiled. He poured the same for Bertie but handed him an American Dry mixer bottle. He poured the same for himself adding, 'we take our ball of Malt straight.., right Muzzy?', who answered, 'the only way.'

Effie eyeing her husband disdainfully.., mouthed, 'about friggin time,' as he poured her drink of Gin and Bitter lemon. He smiled back sweetly at her as she mouthed unsavoury swear words at him.

The other diners were getting in the party spirit.

The waiters clearing the tables with a sense of fulfilment and a service well done. Lots of smiles and grateful thanks from the diners.

Connie and Lena being the youngest moved swiftly around the tables finishing off. Out from the diners bags came the crisps, bottles of lemonade and Tizer for the kids, and the odd bottle of beer for the old man. They were ready for the Dancing.

Bertie signalled to the band for the speciality act.

A drum roll brought Izzey Toke on, in front of the small stage.

"Now for all my fans at the top table, a medley of Al Jolson songs.., I will be appearing without makeup.., 'Oh Naturelle'.., no missus.., take the smile off your face.., my trousers stays on." He went into full Larry Parks actions with..., Swanee, Swanee... The older diners joined in, the Ladies singing and the men miming. With a bit of room in front of the Band he could give his tap dance routine more scope and stretch the number a few extra chorus's. The more adventure's Ladies took to the floor which encouraged the band to give it a right old go. Just before Izzey had his big finish.., Ikey Figgis signalled to his band to go straight into Toot Toot Tootsie Goodbye. Almost the same routine for Izzey apart from shuffled steps to one of the tables near the back, to have a word with an old chap sitting with his Daughter and a couple of kids. The old chap nodded reluctantly. Izzey tap danced his way back in front of the Band finishing off with a couple more choruses.

"Ladies and Gentlemen and Kids.., we have a special treat.., Poplar's very own Song and Dance Man.., star of the 1946 Royal Variety Performance. Appeared in front of the Prince of Wales, King George and other Royal residences to numerous to mention. He's agreed to bless us and do a turn. Come on..., give it up for..., Rex Beamish..,"

Spasmodic clapping encouraging Rex's step and posture to liven up into the dancers usual rhythmic stride..., the old stage magic coming back as he approached Izzey, shaking hands.

Izzey nodded to the Band, they struck up with.

Rockabye Your Baby.., With a Dixie Melody..,

Effie at the top table leant over and whispered .., "Isn't that nice.., the old chap looks good for his age.., mind you where'd he get a name like Rex.?"

"That aint his real name.., its Dick." Said Julian. "You Know who his old man is? They've got that junk shop up the road here.., in Poplar High Street."

"Where'd he get Rex from..,? then, stage name?"

"No.., his Mother always wanted a dog." Julian burst into laughing.., coughing.., spluttering. With all the different food stuffs and now a fair amount of Malt Whiskey the mixture worked its inevitable conclusion.., he shate himself with ominous noise accompaniment. The pained expression on his face told Effie, when she looked at him, its own story. She shrieked with laughter.

"Shut up will you.., you dopey cow. Lester where's the nearest bog?"

"Out that door." he pointed at a door apposite, the other side of the stage. Not thinking Julian crossed in front of the singers trying not to waddle as if he'd shit himself. Effie still creased up with laughter. A few of the other diners had cottoned on and were giggling.

Izzey and Rex carried on with 'April Showers' Izzey carrying most of the tap dancing and singing.., Rex happy to leave any extra bit of stage business to Izzey. The dancers were more numerous enjoying themselves, that's what they came out for so they bleedin.. well were going to.

Izzey and Rex finished their last number and to a ripple of applause they bowed.., As Rex made his way back to his seat a few of the Ladies gave him a kiss on the cheek, his family carried on indifferently chatting between themselves.., without seeming to notice he'd been doing a turn.

The after dinner gossip by the Waiting Staff in the plating room was underway. Everybody relaxed and happy. The music from the band and happy chatter from the dancing diners helped the atmosphere.

Connie grassed the top table up saying they spoke sarcastically about people living in the old houses, just a bunch of slum dwellers in their eyes. They boasted how proud they were of all the slum clearance they engineered. Charlie joined in with what else would you expect off the poisoned dwarfs Julian and his brother George Cuttle.., fishy pair of gits.., if ever there was. Maggie not to miss out on a bit of slandering…, that Effie Cuttle's no better than she should be…, a right, blowsy biddy, And your man.., Mr Seed, fierce kiney toe rag himself..,

Right bunch of article's the whole lot of 'em. Maggie glared around at the others, they very naturally agreed.

Julian's face appeared back at the door, he'd recently scuttled out of.., trying to catch Effie's attention with ppsssed and a wave of his hand.

She eventually went over to him.., barely able to keep from chuckling.

"You can take that grin of your face. I'm in schtuck…, the bleeding stuff's running down the back of my arse, probably ruined my whistle.., not only that the bleeding bogs flooded, all over the floor, I tried in getting there, I reckon I've ruined my shoes, they're soaking wet." Sympathy from Effie., was none existent. She spat.

"Well what do you expect me to do? Put a frigging nappy on you. Shouldn't have been a frigging pig.., should you?"

"Don't you start.., that's all I need. Tell Muzzy I need him."

Effie wended her way slowly in between the dancers stopping to chat to some of her friends. Knowing full well that her old man was going spare. At the table she explained to Lester Seed and Bertie Roseman, Julian's plight, they all looked over to see him animated waving his hand vigorously to come over. Bertie started to get up but Lester put his hand on his shoulder, instead, rose abruptly, too quickly. Julian's predicament, with the same ominous noise but a much more gentlemanly expression from Mr Seed.

"Oh dear.., pardon me I seem to have had a mishap. If you'll excuse me." Lester Seed moved as fast as he dared across to join Julian. An animated conversation between them led to the pair of them seeking help.

Effie meanwhile had coerced Bertie into dancing the twist, reluctantly he had to be dragged onto the floor. But enthusiastically once the mood got him.

Lester Seed luckily had a spare pair of trousers in his office on the second floor, he always changed into a pair of old trousers when he had to go on a site inspection. He sneakily used the Ladies toilet on that floor to clean himself up.

Julian was left to his own devices. He had to go out to the road by the Town Hall..., Woodstock Terrace. He'd left his shiny Jaguar car outside one of his workers sisters house, Joyce Trent. He'd paid a couple of her kids to look after his prized possession, his Jaguar. He got one of the kids to go and borrow a pair of their Fathers old trousers. He had to then tell a few porkies.., to Joyce.., problems with his kidneys.., eventually he got some help.., but it cost him.

Word got back to Doreen, in the plating room.., about the top table having the 'two bob bits. Paying the Waiters off for the nights work.

"All the eating irons and plates stashed away? Charlie..," She asked

"All tickady boo. Your highness." He chirruped back, "And the slops taken care of."

"Shame the nobs got 'Gandhi's' revenge.., still, old Gandhi did like us cockney's."

They all looked at Charlie.., who smiled benignly.

"Dad?" asked Connie, "What you been up to?"

Charlie with a Stan Laurel smile innocently asked.., "What Me?"

Raising his eyebrows and turning his head innocently.

Doreen and her staff giving Charlie the old fashioned grin and shake of the heads and 'get him' expression.

A cough and "Hello.., Hello.., Hello." Startled them. "Whats going on here.., then." Worriedly they turned to see Sergeant Rivett laughing his head off. "Gets em every time…,"

Doreen stammered "Sergeant.., Ron.., you made us jump.., what can we do for you?"

"Funny old business with Mr Seed and 'flash harry' Julian Cuttle getting took short. Must have been the drink because I had a spoonful of Caviar and a Jellied Eel. Nothing wrong with me, nothing wrong with Effie either.., I see she out doing the Twist, with the other bloke on their table, her great 'arris' likely to knock someone over if they get in the way. Only come to see Chas.., did you do that favour for me .?"

Smiling at the Sergeant. Charlie handed him a substantial package.

"Cheers Chas..," Then he looked at Doreen. "You don't mind?"

"Anything for my favourite copper." She winked flirtily.

He tapped his forehead. "Goodnight all, Mind how you go…," The Ikey Figgis Band still going strong with plenty of noise feeling.

A sunny Sunday afternoon in Shadwell Park. Connie convinced Lena and Hettie that a kickabout with a tennis ball in the park would help digest Sunday dinner. Sorting a place on the grass to play in, Hettie's shopping bag would be one goalpost and Connie's cap and coat would be the other. The goalie was Hettie, Connie centre forward and Lena defender. Play started with Connie, ball at his feet being tricky and lairey rolling the ball temptingly under his foot, he then pirouetted slowly giving Lena the chance to get a tackle in which she excepted with glee by hacking Connie's legs from under him, he went arse over tip landing on his back holding his ankle in pain, Lena dribbled the ball and scored past Hettie. The two Ladies shaking and hugging with laughter. Connie shouting ' refer.. ree' indignantly.

Hettie announcing, 'four nil to Lena,' adding 'get up you big slomacky sod... for Gawd Sake!!!'

*